Ray

The Stone Dragon

Cover art adapted from an original painting
by

Hamish Hebben

1

Author's Note

This is a work of fiction. Names, characters, businesses, places, events and incidents are either the products of the author's imagination or used in a fictitious manner. Any resemblance to actual persons, living or dead, or actual events is purely coincidental.

Contents

For Hamish,

*whose painting inspired me
to write this story.*

Chapter One: The Prisoner

It all began because Timothy Tamworth's neighbour kept birds in a big shed in his back garden. Timothy could see the roof of the shed on the other side of his garden fence, and he'd often wondered what his neighbour, Mr Fowler, kept in it, but he didn't find out until one sunny Friday morning in the summer holidays when he was eleven years old.

Timothy and his friend David were out in Timothy's garden, playing a game that they'd invented themselves: a game that was a bit like tennis. They had a length of blue plastic rope tied up between two poles spaced about four metres apart. They called it 'soft-ball' tennis. They used tennis racquets, but the ball was a soft, yellow sponge ball instead of a tennis ball. That was mainly because if you hit a tennis ball hard it can go flying off a long way, and Timothy's garden wasn't big enough for that.

The rules of their game were slightly different to proper tennis. The idea was to stop the ball from touching the ground. If the ball touched the ground on your opponent's side of the rope, you scored a point. If the ball touched the ground on your side of the rope, your opponent scored a point, but the ball had to go over the top of the rope. If it went under the rope and touched the ground, it didn't count.

'What's the game going to be today then, Tim?' David had asked when he arrived in Timothy's back garden.

'We'll play five points to a set, and five sets for the match. Is that okay with you?'

'Yeah, fine. Beat me if you can, loser.'

Timothy grinned. They had been friends ever since they first started going to junior school, and when this summer holiday was over, they would be going to the same high school. They were both good players at this game they'd made up together, and because of it a friendly rivalry had developed between them. There was always a good deal of jokey banter involved when one of them scored a point against the other, but no matter who won or lost they always had a laugh about it and remained friends afterwards.

After they had played for about an hour, the score stood at two sets each, so the fifth set would decide who won the match. Making his next serve, David gave the ball an almighty whack that sent it flying over the fence into the neighbour's garden. It bounced off the roof of the big shed and disappeared.

'We can't leave it at that, Tim, can we?' David said. 'We've won two sets each, so everything depends on the fifth set. You'll just have to go and get the ball back so we can finish the game.'

Timothy wasn't very fond of his neighbour. He was a grumpy old man who didn't seem to like children very much, but it was important to get that ball back and finish the match, so he summoned his courage and went around to his neighbour's house.

As he walked down the path to his neighbour's front door, he was unaware that getting that ball back was going to lead him on the most amazing adventure. He would look back one day and realise that if David hadn't sent that ball over his neighbour's fence on that sunny summer morning, the events that followed would probably never had happened.

Feeling just a little bit nervous, Timothy knocked on his neighbour's front door. After a moment or two the door opened and there stood bad-tempered Mr. Fowler looking down at him. 'Oh, it's you, is it?' he said. 'What do you want?'

'I'm sorry to bother you, Mr Fowler,' said Timothy, 'but me and my friend were playing with a ball and it's just gone over the fence into your garden. Would you let me go and find it, please?'

'You want to be more careful, then. Them footballs can do a lot of damage, knock plants down and break windows.'

'It's not a football, Mr Fowler, it's just a little sponge ball. It's not heavy enough to do any damage. It's bright yellow, so it shouldn't be too hard to find.'

'Hmm. Well, all right, then. You can go and find it. Go through the side gate and down the path. But you be careful not to damage any of my plants, and don't kick it over into my garden again because next time I might not let you have it back.'

Timothy couldn't understand why Mr Fowler was being so nasty about it, but he told himself that there was no point in getting upset. The important thing to do was go and find the ball, then take it back to his own garden so that he and David could finish their game.

Mr Fowler's garden was about the same size as his own, but much tidier. There was a patch of carefully mown lawn with flower borders all round it, and beyond that was a vegetable garden with runner beans, potatoes, leeks, carrots and cabbages all neatly laid out in straight rows. At the side of the garden, close to the fence between Mr Fowler's garden and his own, stood that big, long shed.

As he walked down the garden looking for his ball, he

noticed that there were two windows in the side of the shed facing the garden, and that both of them had been opened slightly. He saw that there were double doors in the end of the shed that faced towards the house, and like the windows, both of them were very slightly open.

He found his sponge ball easily. It was lying on the ground between two rows of runner beans. He picked it up, being very careful not to damage any of the bean plants, or tread on anything. On his way back again, he thought he'd just take a quick peek through the doors of that shed to see what was inside. He hadn't meant to go into the shed at all, but when he saw inside it, he just couldn't help himself.

On long worktops, on both side of the shed, were rows of wooden cages, and in each one was a number of small, brightly coloured birds. Each cage had a wire netting front with a glass water bottle fixed to it, plastic feeder trays with bird seed and pellets in them, and perches for the birds to sit on. All the cages were clean and tidy, and the little birds fluttered and

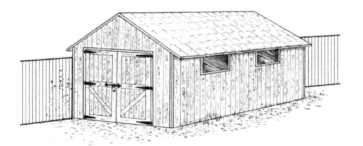

twittered as he walked past them. He noticed that, in the wall of the shed that was closest to the garden fence, there was just one small window. But what really caught his attention was a very odd-looking bird in a cage down the end of the shed against the back wall. He'd never seen anything quite so strange in all his life. It was much bigger than any of the other birds, in fact it was so big that there was hardly enough room in its cage for it to turn around.

Certainly, it looked a bit like a bird. Its body was covered in what looked like very thin, fine feathers – brownish on its back and sides; grey on its chest and tummy. It had wings folded across its back, and it stood on two legs like a bird, with very big claws like an eagle's talons on its feet, but it was the most peculiar bird he had ever seen. It had a long tail covered in very small feathers that looked more like a rat's tail than a bird's, and a very long neck. Timothy knew that it wasn't unusual for birds to have long necks. Swans and geese, for example, have very long necks too. But its head was very different from a bird's head, because there were two long, backward-pointing horns on the top of it, and where a bird has a beak, this strange creature didn't have a beak at all. It had a mouth, and in that mouth, there were teeth like needles.

'I don't know what that is,' thought Timothy, 'but I'm quite sure it isn't a bird. Birds don't have teeth.'

As he stood there staring at it, a feeling of sadness came over him. This creature, whatever it was, wasn't fluttering about and chirping like the other birds. It just sat there looking lost and alone. When it lifted up its head and looked directly at him, Timothy saw that it had something else that no bird ever had. It had bright blue eyes that seemed to glow with intelligence. It was in that moment that he first heard a squeaky voice that seemed to be coming from the cage.

The voice said, 'Please help me, Timothy. I need your help to get out of here. I want to go home.'

Timothy was so startled that he staggered backwards, tripped over a plastic bucket, and sat down heavily on his bottom on the hard floor. For a moment or two he was afraid to move at all, but he got up off the floor when the voice said, 'Get up, Timothy. Please. Get up and let me out.' At the same time, the strange-looking bird pulled at the wire netting front of its cage with one of its clawed feet. Timothy, curiosity overcoming his earlier shock, was just about to take a closer look at the creature when Mr Fowler appeared in the doorway of the shed.

'What are you doing in my shed, boy?' he said angrily. 'I let you look for your ball and now you're sneaking about disturbing my birds. You haven't any business to be in there. Come on, out of it. Now!'

Timothy turned away from the cage with the strange bird in it, and moved towards the door.

'I see you've found your ball, so take it and go. But remember what I said. If you kick it over the fence again, you won't be getting it back.'

That made Timothy feel quite angry. He hadn't meant to cause any trouble, and he'd been very careful not

13

to damage or break anything. He'd been polite, he'd tried to be friendly, and he hadn't actually kicked the ball anyway. But Timothy's father had always taught him never to return anger with anger. He'd said, 'If someone's angry with you, Tim, try not be angry back. Always stay calm and reasonable, and if you can't do anything else, just walk away and say nothing.'

Walking away and saying nothing didn't seem right, so Timothy said, 'I'm sorry if I've upset you, Mr Fowler. I didn't mean to. The shed door was open, and I couldn't help noticing all these lovely birds. I just wanted to take a look at them. I didn't think you'd mind.'

That seemed to calm the old man down a bit. 'Oh, well … all right then,' he said. 'You haven't done any harm, I suppose, but you ought to have asked me first before you came in here.'

'Well then, I'm sorry about that too, Mr Fowler. What sort of bird is that browny-grey one in that cage down at the end there?'

'Ah, that's a very rare and valuable bird, that is. Worth a lot of money, I shouldn't wonder. If people knew it was here, there might be some who'd try to steal it from me.'

'So that's why he's angry,' thought Timothy. 'He doesn't want anyone to know he's got that strange bird-that's-not-a-bird in his shed. He's frightened someone might try to take it away.'

'I won't say anything, Mr Fowler, I promise. I

wouldn't want anyone to steal any of your birds. All I want is to get my ball back so me and my friend can finish our game.'

'All right. You've found your ball, so off you go, and we'll say no more about it.'

When Timothy lost the final set 4-1, David said, 'You feeling all right, mate? You played that last set like an idiot. It's no fun beating you when you don't even try.'

Before Timothy could answer, they heard Timothy's mother call through the kitchen window.

'Is David staying for lunch, Tim? I can make you some sandwiches if you want, and I got some nice, fresh Danish pastries from the shop this morning.'

'That's very kind of you, Mrs Tamworth,' David called back, 'but my mum said she wants me home for lunch because we're going out this afternoon.'

'Where are you off to this afternoon, then?' asked Timothy.

'Oh, my mum's taking me to Thenmans, the outfitters, to get my uniform for high school. I expect your mum'll be doing the same soon.'

'Yeah, I expect so,' said Tim in a half-hearted sort of way.

David gave his friend a puzzled look.

'Something's upset you, hasn't it? You were all right before you went to get the ball back. Did something happen next door?'

Timothy almost began to tell his best friend about the strange bird-like creature, but then he remembered that he'd promised Mr Fowler he wouldn't do that.

'Oh, it's just that he's got lots of birds in cages in his shed.'

'So? Lots of people keep birds: budgies and parrots and things, Tim. They're probably his pets.'

'That's just it, David. They're not pets, they're prisoners. It's not right, keeping birds in cages. They ought to be free to fly around, and build nests, and lay eggs and eat worms and insects and stuff. I don't like to see birds shut up in cages. They can't be happy cooped up like that, can they? It's just not natural.'

'You know, you can be a bit of a wally at times, Tim,' said David with an amused smile.

Timothy shrugged. 'Maybe you'd rather not have a wally for a friend, then.'

'Don't be silly. We're mates, and we always will be, right? If you have a few odd ideas now and then, it's okay with me. Tell you what, next time we'll play in my garden and then there won't be any birds for you to worry about. Okay?'

Timothy nodded. 'Yeah, ok.'

'Right, see you, then.'

'Yeah, see you.'

After David had gone home, Timothy wandered up to his bedroom to sit down on the swivel chair in front of his computer desk. He had hoped that he and his friend would be able to spend the afternoon playing a car racing game. He began to set up a single-player game, but he found that his heart wasn't in it. He just couldn't concentrate: he couldn't get the events of that morning out of his mind.

Now that he was back in his own bedroom, the strange creature in the cage next door seemed unreal. Had that squeaky voice really been the creature talking to him, or was it just his imagination?

Timothy liked reading books. One of his favourite subjects was history. There were lots of books in his bedroom – two small bookcases full of them, a pile of books on his dressing table and another pile on the floor that he hadn't been able to put anywhere else. He picked up one of the books off the floor. It was a book about dinosaurs. He'd been very much into dinosaurs when he was younger. He flipped through the pages with his finger, and stopped suddenly when he saw a picture of a flying dinosaur. It was called a Pterosaur. It had a long beak like a bird. It didn't have any feathers so far as he could see, nor a very long tail, and it had only one big horn on the back of its head, but it did look the same sort of shape as the creature he'd seen in his neighbour's shed. He put the book down and went to stand at his bedroom window, from where he could see the shed in his neighbour's garden. 'It can't be a Pterosaur,' he thought. 'Pterosaurs lived on the earth millions of years ago. There aren't any Pterosaurs left anymore, so it's not one of those.'

A Pterosaur

Then he remembered how forlorn and sad the creature had looked. He remembered those bright, blue eyes and the intelligence that seemed to shine out of them. 'That voice was real,' he said to himself. 'That little creature is unhappy in that cage. It doesn't belong there. It wants to be free to fly away home, wherever that is. It asked for my help, and I'm not going to turn my back on it. I'm going to get it out of that cage and let it go.'

Timothy knew there would be trouble when Mr Fowler found that the creature was gone. 'He'll be angry and he'll probably phone the police,' he thought. 'Then they'll come around here and ask questions. They'll want to know if I had anything to do with it. Well, I'm not going to lie. I'll own up and take whatever punishment they decide to give me. After all, it's not as though I'll be stealing the creature to keep it for myself, and if letting it go free is really such a bad thing to do, then keeping it a prisoner in a cage is a worse one.'

He sat down at his computer desk and began to make a plan. 'If it really can talk,' he thought, 'I'll ask it where it came from, and how it ended up in that cage in Mr Fowler's shed. Then I'll let it fly away home. What I need to do is figure out how I'm going to do that without getting caught.'

Chapter Two: A Bad Word

Later that afternoon, Timothy looked at his bedside clock and realised that it was almost dinner time. His father usually arrived home from his office job at the local council about 6pm, and the clock said 5.45.

He ran down the stairs into the kitchen. 'What's for dinner, mum?'

'I got five nice salmon fillets from the shop this morning, and I grilled three of them earlier, so we'll have them cold with salad. I'll put the other two fillets in the fridge and make fishcakes with them tomorrow.'

Timothy was pleased with that because he liked salad, especially on hot summer days, and he just loved his mother's fishcakes, so that was something to look forward to the next day. He went back upstairs to wash his hands, and then hurried down again to help his mother by laying the table with place mats, knives, forks, spoons, paper napkins, and a drizzler bottle of salad dressing so that everything would be ready when his father came in.

While the three of them were eating their dinner, Timothy told his father what he'd been doing that day, about the soft-ball tennis game he played with his friend, and how David couldn't stay for lunch because his mother was taking him to get fitted out with new school uniform. He didn't say anything about his neighbour's shed, about the birds in the cages, or the strange-looking one.

'Are you and David looking forward to going to your new school then, Tim?' his father asked.

'Yes, dad. They've got a big sports hall there, and two proper tennis courts outside, so we'll be able to learn to play tennis properly.'

Timothy and his parents had been invited to have a look around the High School on Open Night, a couple of weeks before. They'd met some of the teachers, including Miss Henderson, who would be Timothy's form teacher, and Mr Tennison, the sports teacher who taught football, cricket, and tennis. David and his parents had been there too.

'So, you're both going to take up playing tennis when you get there?'

'You bet. We might even be able to get in the school team.'

'Is there a tennis team at the school, then?'

'I don't know, but there will be when me and David get there.'

'That, my boy, is a very good attitude. Your sports master, Mr Tennison, will like that.'

Mr Tamworth leaned across the table and pointed a finger at his son.

'Mr Tennison teaches tennis, to David, Timothy and Dennis,' he said with a grin.

Timothy's mother rolled her eyes up at the ceiling. Timothy looked at his father and scowled.

His father stared back at him. 'What?'

'You said "Dennis" '.

'What's wrong with "Dennis"? I only said it because Timothy and David don't rhyme with tennis.'

'I know that, Dad, but to me, "Dennis" is a bad word.'

'Is it? Why's that, then?'

'Well … there's this big kid in our class. His name's Dennis Parker. No one likes him very much. He doesn't wear school uniform. He always wears jeans and a tee shirt, and trainers. He's a bit of a bully, and he's always making fun of David and me because we like tennis and he likes football. He says only girls play tennis.'

'Well, that's not true, is it? There's a famous tennis champion with the same name as you, and he's definitely not a girl.'

'Yes, Dad, I know that too. Dennis only says things like that to try to make me look silly in front of the other kids.'

'Has this Dennis boy ever hit you, Tim?' asked his mother.

'He's punched me a couple of times. He gets angry when he tries to upset me and it doesn't work.'

'Does he do the same thing with David?'

'He calls David names, but he's never punched him because he's afraid David would hit him back. One day, Dennis started calling me a sissy girl, but I just turned around and walked away like Dad said. He punched me in the back. He was going to do it again, but David stepped between us. He didn't say anything, he just stood there staring at Dennis. Then Dennis called him a girl too, and David said he didn't mind being called a girl because girls are as good as boys any day. Dennis didn't know what to say to that, so then he walked away.'

'Your friend David had the right idea. What he did was both very brave and very thoughtful. I've always told you that it's wrong to hit people, haven't I?' said Mr Tamworth.

'Yes, Dad. I wouldn't want to hit anyone anyway.'

'Well, Tim, it sounds like this Dennis isn't a very nice person. But two good things have come out of it. It's good that you've told me and your mum about it, and it's good that we've sat and talked about it because, when you've got problems, that's always the best way to go about solving them.'

'David and me talked about it too. He says not to worry, because things might be different at high school. Dennis Parker isn't all that bright, so he might not even be in the same class as us.'

'David might well be right. But if this Dennis Parker makes a nuisance of himself at high school, I want you to tell me and your mum about it. Will you do that?'

'Yes, Dad. I will if you promise me you won't go to the school and start making a fuss, because that'll make me look silly, and it'll probably just make

Dennis Parker more angry.'

'Ok. If things get any worse for you, I'll just have a quiet word with your form teacher, Miss Henderson. She seems to be a very capable lady, and I'm sure she'd know the best way to handle it. There's no reason why anyone other than us three here and Miss Henderson should know anything about it.'

Timothy nodded. 'All right.'

'So, we understand each other, agreed?'

'Yes, Dad. Agreed.'

When Timothy had helped his mother to wash up and dry the dishes, he asked his father if there was going to be anything interesting on TV that evening. His father said no, and that he had some reading to do anyway, which was what Timothy was hoping for. 'I'll go up and play a game on my computer, then, and see if there's any emails for me,' he said.

'Ok, Tim. Come down and say goodnight when it's bedtime.'

'Ok, Dad.'

Back in his bedroom, Timothy continued making his plan. It was going to be a warm, sticky night, so he would leave his window open. He would normally close his bedroom door, but tonight he would leave it almost, but not quite, closed. He found a torch, checked to see that it worked properly, and placed it on his bedside table next to his battery alarm clock. The clock made a beep-beep noise when the alarm went off. It wasn't very loud, and he didn't think his parents would hear it, but just to be on the safe side he tucked it under his pillow.

He set the alarm for one o'clock in the morning, because it would be pitch dark then, and everyone would be fast asleep. He took off his clothes and put on his pyjamas. He folded his clothes into a neat pile on a chair, placing them in the right order so that he could dress easily in the dark, and put his soft-soled trainers under the chair. He looked around and decided there was nothing more he could do for the time being, so he switched his computer on. There were three emails from school friends eager to tell him about where they were, or where they'd been, and what they'd been doing on their holidays, so he settled down to read, and answer them.

Chapter 3: Shakes and Ladders

Timothy went downstairs to say goodnight to his parents. Then he went back to his bedroom, and got into bed. He expected that it would be quite difficult to get to sleep knowing that he was about to do something that would probably get him into a great deal of trouble. So he was quite surprised when his alarm clock went *beep-beep* underneath his pillow.

He rolled over, grabbed the torch from his bedside table, pulled out the clock from under his pillow and quickly switched the alarm off. By the light of his torch he could see that it was one o'clock in the morning.

For a moment or two he lay quite still, listening to see if either of his parents had been woken by the alarm, but there were no sounds of doors opening or of footsteps on the landing, so he eased himself carefully out of bed and got dressed.

Looking out of his window he could see that it was really dark outside. The sky was clear: he could see some stars. The night was still and silent, and a bright moon was almost full. He pulled on his trainers and laced them.

Timothy opened his bedroom door just enough so that he could see his parents' bedroom door across the landing. It was closed and there was no sound from beyond it. Using his torch to light the steps so that he wouldn't fall over, he crept carefully down the stairs and around into the kitchen. By the light of his torch, he crossed the kitchen to carefully unlock the back door. He pushed the door open, switched off the torch and stuffed it into his pocket.

Lying against the wall opposite the kitchen door was his father's two-part ladder. It had a wide section and a narrow section that slid together to make a long ladder. He picked up the wide section of the ladder, carried it across the garden, and set it against the garden fence. Then he went back for the narrow section of the ladder, setting that against the fence close beside the wide part.

He climbed slowly up the wide section of the ladder, sat down astride the fence, then reached down to take hold of the narrow section. This was the most dangerous part of his plan because anyone looking out of the upstairs windows of either his house, or Mr Fowler's, would be able to see him quite easily.

Looking down between the big shed and the fence he could see that the gap between them was only about a metre wide. 'It'll be a bit of a squeeze climbing down,' he said to himself, 'but I think I can probably do it.' He noticed again the single, small window in that side of the shed.

Very slowly and carefully he lifted the narrow section of the ladder, using both hands to raise it little by little until it was high enough to swing over the fence without hitting anything, then he lowered it gently down into the gap between the fence and the shed. He was so worried that he might make a noise lifting and lowering the ladder that, when it was done, he found himself shaking a little even though the night was still very warm. He paused for a moment, taking several deep breaths to calm himself, before he climbed down into his neighbour's garden.

The first thing he did was to creep around to the double door at the end of the shed to see if it was still open, but he found it closed, with a big, brass padlock holding it shut. He went back to take a closer look at the single window in the side of the shed that faced towards the fence, to find it had been left slightly open. 'That's probably so that the birds can get a bit of fresh air,' he thought.

The small window wasn't as high off the ground as the windows at the front of the shed, but it was too high up for him to just climb into. He thought about it for a moment and realised that, if he climbed up the narrow part of the ladder, and then turned around to face the window, he would be at the right level to open the window fully, lean forward, and crawl through it. A moment or two later he found himself, on his hands and knees, on top of the wooden bird cages that stood on the worktop under the window.

'I hope these cages are strongly made,' he thought. 'I'd hate to injure any of the little birds by falling on them.'

As he jumped down onto the floor of the shed, the squeaky voice said, 'Hello, Timothy. I knew you'd come back, and I'm very pleased to see you again.'

Timothy moved down to the end of the shed where the strange creature's cage was. He bent down and peered into it.

'What are you? Where did you come from?'

'I'm a dragon. My home is in Dragonworld.'

'A … a dragon? I thought dragons were great big things.'

'They are, Timothy.'

'Then, why are you so small?'

'There's an awful lot of things I have to explain to you, but we don't have time for it right now. Just open the cage and let me out.'

The front of the cage was hinged at one side, with a simple wooden turnbuckle holding it closed. Timothy twisted the turnbuckle around and pulled the front of the cage open.

'Stand aside,' said the dragon, 'I'm going to fly up onto the ledge of that little window behind you.'

Timothy moved to one side as the little creature put its head out of the cage and spread its wings.

'Goodness!' thought Timothy, 'I didn't realise its wings were that big. They're longer than its body and neck put together!'

The little dragon jumped up out of the cage, flapped his wings, and landed on the sill of the small window.

'I'm going to hop across and sit on top of the fence,' it said. 'I'll keep watch while you climb back out of the window, and I'll warn you if there's anyone coming.'

The tops of the bird cages that stood underneath the small window were too high off the floor for Timothy to just step up onto them. He looked around and saw the plastic bucket that he had tripped over the day before. He turned it upside down and stood on it. With that extra bit of height, he was able to scramble back up on top of the cages without disturbing the little birds too much.

He crawled through the window head first and, grasping the rungs of the ladder with both hands, he pulled himself up onto it. Then he twisted around to push the small window until it was just slightly open again. As he swung a foot over the fence onto the wide part of the ladder, he realised that the dragon had disappeared.

'That's odd,' Timothy thought, 'because it said it wanted to explain things. Maybe it's changed its mind. Oh well, I've done what I set out to do. It's free now. I just hope it gets home safely. I wonder where Dragonworld is?'

And then, with one leg either side of the fence, he froze because a light had just come on in his neighbour's kitchen.

'Oh, no!' he whispered to himself, 'Mr Fowler's woken up! He'll be out here in a minute!' In a sudden panic he pulled the narrow part of the ladder back over fence so quickly that it caught the edge of the shed roof with a metallic 'clang'. Desperate to get down out of sight, Timothy dropped the narrow part of the ladder onto his lawn, where it made an even louder clang, and jumped down onto the grass.

'Don't move, Timothy,' whispered the squeaky voice. Stay close to the fence. He can't see you and he can't see the ladder. Keep still, keep quiet, and he won't know you're here.'

'I thought you'd gone. I thought you'd flown away home,' Timothy whispered back.

'I can't get home without your help, Timothy, so I'm going to look after you. Trust me, everything will be all right.'

Timothy heard his neighbour's back door open, and then he saw the glow of a torch coming down the garden path. There was a rattling sound.

'He's checking the padlock on the shed door,' whispered the dragon, and then, 'Now he's looking to see if the windows are still as he left them before he went to bed.'

A few moments later, the dragon said, 'He's going back indoors now. Don't move yet. I'll tell you when it's safe.'

Timothy stood by the fence trying not to move or make any sound for what seemed quite a long time, but was probably only about five minutes. When the light in Mr Fowler's kitchen went out, the little dragon said, 'It's ok now, Timothy, your neighbour's gone back to bed. He won't be getting up any more until the morning.'

Timothy picked up the narrow ladder and carried it back to the wall by the back door, and then returned for the wide one. Having put the ladders back exactly as they were when he found them, he opened the back door, went inside, and locked it. Then he crept slowly and carefully up the stairs to his bedroom. When he got there, he found the dragon sitting on his bedroom windowsill. It was the first time that Timothy had been able to have a good look at it.

'Do you have a name?' he asked.

'Dragons don't use names in the same way that humans do, Timothy, because among ourselves, we don't need to. But a very long time ago, in another part of your world, humans used to call me Menhir. The language those people spoke was called Breton, and in that language, Menhir means "Longstone".'

'Why did they call you that?

'Because I'm a stone dragon.'

'A stone dragon? But you're not made of stone, are you?

'No indeed, Timothy. I'm flesh, and blood, and bones just like you are, although my bones are hollow where yours are solid. There are two other types of dragon in Dragonworld, but the stone dragons are the biggest and strongest of them all. We're called stone dragons because we can lift and carry big, heavy stones.'

'What other kinds of dragon are there?'

'In my world, there are stone dragons, sea dragons and flame dragons.'

'Flame dragons? Wow! Are they the ones that snort fire down their noses and burn houses down, and stuff?'

That was the first time that Timothy ever heard a

dragon laugh. It sounded like *hurrr-hurrr-hurrr* and Menhir's head bobbed up and down as he did it.

'No, no, Timothy. That's just a silly story that humans made up because most of you have never seen a dragon, and those few of you that have seen one don't remember it. Flame dragons are the smallest and fastest of dragons. They are so called because their plumage is red and orange and gold. When they come diving down at great speed to grab a fish out of the sea, with the sunlight flashing and sparkling off their red-gold feathers, they look like flames falling from the sky.'

'How could someone see a dragon and not remember it, Menhir? I certainly won't forget you.'

'No, Timothy, you won't. But before we go into that I must have something to eat. I haven't had any real food for weeks. I'm starving, and I'm feeling very weak. It was all I could do to fly up onto your window sill. I need food.'

'What do dragons eat?'

'Raw meat sometimes, but fish mostly. There's some fish in your mother's fridge. Could you get it for me?'

'How do you know there's fish in my mum's fridge?'

'Get me the fish first, and then I'll tell you.'

'But my mum and dad might wake up if I go downstairs again.'

'No, they won't. Trust me. Dragons don't lie.'

'Don't they? Why not?'

'Humans lie when they're afraid of something, but dragons aren't afraid of anything. There's nothing in either your world or mine that can hurt a dragon so we never have any need to lie. Besides, it's simply not possible for a dragon to lie.'

'That sounds odd, Menhir. Surely anyone can lie if they want to. Why can't dragons do it?'

'There's lots of other, more important things, you'll need to know before I can explain about that.'

'All right. I'll go and get the fish.'

Menhir

The Stone Dragon

Chapter 4: Rainbows and Moonbows

Menhir was right. Timothy walked down the stairs without bothering to be particularly quiet about it, but his parents didn't wake up. He opened the fridge. The two pieces of salmon that his mother was going to make into fishcakes were in a plastic box. He picked the box up, took an empty supermarket carrier bag from the cupboard under the sink, and took them back to his bedroom.

'I don't want you making a smelly, fishy mess on my bedroom floor, Menhir,' he said, 'so I'll put your food on this plastic bag.'

The dragon held one of the salmon fillets down with his clawed foot, tore a piece off it with his teeth, tipped his head back, and gulped it down.

'Oooh, this really tasty, Timothy,' he said,' I love salmon.'

'So do I,' said Timothy, 'but my mum's going to make an awful fuss when she finds out it's gone. And Mr Fowler's going to make a fuss too, when he finds out your cage is empty.'

'You don't have to worry about that,' said Menhir between bites, 'because your mother won't remember that she had any salmon in her fridge, and your neighbour won't remember that he ever had a strange bird in his shed.'

'What? How can that be?'

Menhir stopped eating for a moment.

'I said that I've got a lot of things to explain to you, Timothy, but if you look at your clock, you'll see that it's now three o'clock in the morning, and you need to get some sleep.'

'Oh, but that's not fair! I helped you escape from that awful cage, and now I want to know all about you, Menhir. I want to know where you come from and how you got here. I want to know how you ended up in that cage, and most of all, I want to know why my mum and Mr Fowler won't remember things.'

'You're right, Timothy,' said the dragon, 'I owe you a debt for helping me to escape, and I will repay you for it. But first, you have to find a way to help me get back to my home in Dragonworld. To do that, you will have to understand how I came to be here in your world. But you need sleep too, so I'll make a bargain with you. Get your pyjamas on and get into bed, and then I'll tell you the story of how dragons first found their way into your world. When I've finished the story, you must go to sleep. Everything else you need to know, I'll tell you about tomorrow. Agreed?'

Timothy nodded. 'All right.' He got undressed, put his pyjamas on, and snuggled down in his bed.

'A long, long time ago,' began Menhir, 'a dragon called Rhyol was flying around one night when there was a bright, full moon in the sky. He was near a place where a river of red-hot molten lava flows out from a volcano and down into the sea. When lava reaches the sea, it makes huge clouds of steam that rise way up into the sky. Rhyol looked up through that cloud of steam and he saw a coloured ring around the moon. It's called a Moonbow.'

'I've never heard of a Moonbow,' said Timothy. 'Is it anything like a rainbow?'

'Yes,' said Menhir, 'the two things are very similar. A rainbow is caused by the sun shining through tiny droplets of water in the air. That's why you see a rainbow when it's raining and the sun is shining at the same time.

'A Moonbow is caused by the moon shining through tiny droplets of water in the air too, so it happens on foggy nights, or when you're near a place where mist rises from the sea, or near a waterfall, or a lake. A Moonbow isn't as bright as a rainbow, and the colours are usually just yellow and orange. While Rhyol was looking at the Moonbow, he saw something very odd, something that no dragon had ever seen before. The colour of the Moonbow turned blue.

'Rhyol was puzzled, so he flew directly at the Moonbow to try to find out why it had changed colour. All of a sudden, he found himself surrounded by a tunnel of white light. Inside the tunnel a howling wind was blowing that pushed him along. After a few moments he came out of the tunnel to find himself flying over a world that was quite unlike his own.

'Dragonworld, you see, is a vast ocean with lots of rocky islands poking up out of it. On some of those islands there are volcanoes, and rivers of lava flowing into the sea. In Dragonworld, dragons are the only creatures that can fly: there aren't any birds there. On some of the larger islands there are creatures that walk on four legs. They look a bit like the dinosaurs in your book. But the world that Rhyol looked down on was very different. It had woodlands with lots of different kinds of trees, grassy green hills, and beautiful flowers. There were birds flying in the sky, lots and lots of different kinds of small, furry animals running about on the ground, and all of them were strange to him.'

'Aren't there any trees or grass in Dragonworld then, Menhir?'

'Yes, there are, but not like the trees and grass in your world. Do you know what a fern is?'

'Yes, they grow in damp places in woodland, and on heathland too, I think.'

'That's right, Timothy,' said Menhir. 'In Dragonworld the trees look like giant ferns, and the grass is much taller and thicker than it is in your world; it's more like bamboo. It grows so high that someone as small as you would get lost in it.

'Rhyol was fascinated by this strange new world in which he found himself but, because he was a dragon, he wasn't frightened. He wanted to know more about it.

'Looking back at the Moonbow, he could still see Dragonworld at the other end of the tunnel of light, but he didn't know why that tunnel had appeared, or how long it would last. He thought that, maybe, if he stayed too long in this new world, the tunnel might

A Fern plant

A Fern Tree

disappear and then he'd never be able to get back to his own world.

'So, he very quickly found some great big rocks, picked them up, and set them down in a circle to mark the place where the tunnel of light came out. When he'd finished doing that, he tried to fly back into the tunnel of light to return to Dragonworld so that he could set down some more stones to mark where the tunnel began. But what he found was that the very strong, roaring wind that carried him easily from Dragonworld into your world was now blowing against him, so that getting back from your world to Dragonworld against the force of that wind was much more difficult. Rhyol was a very strong, fully-grown stone dragon, but even so, he had to work extremely hard to fight against the strength of that wind.

'Once he was back in Dragonworld he collected some more big rocks and arranged them in a circle where the blue Moonbow had formed, so that he could easily find the same place again. Then he flew off to tell the other dragons about it.'

'Did the other dragons believe him, Menhir?' asked Timothy.

'Yes, they did, because dragons don't lie. But they were very puzzled. All of them had seen Moonbows before, but none of them had ever seen a Moonbow turn blue. Two more stone dragons, called Graphir and Arkos, flew back with Rhyol to the stone circle he'd made, but by the time they got there, the Moonbow had gone. They sat around the circle and talked, trying to make sense of what Rhyol had told them.

'After a short while, a very old and wise flame dragon called Kalmandar flew down to join them. He listened very carefully to what Rhyol had to say, and to the opinions of the other two stone dragons. Then he said that he thought the blue Moonbow was a kind of gateway in space and time. He called it a Portal, and he said that the portal probably wouldn't open again until there was another bright, full moon.

'Now, all dragons know that there's only a full moon once every twenty-eight days. So, they all agreed to meet back at the stone circle twenty seven days later to see what might happen.'

'And did the portal open again, Menhir?' asked Timothy.

'Yes, Timothy, it did. This time all three of the stone dragons went through the portal into the new world.'

'Did Kalmandar the flame dragon go too?'

'No, because Rhyol had warned him about the howling wind that blows from Dragonworld into your world. Flame dragons are only half as big as stone dragons, and nothing like as strong. If Kalmandar had gone through the portal, he wouldn't have been strong enough to fly back again.'

'So, Rhyol, Graphir and Arkos went through the portal, then?'

'Yes, Timothy, they did, but only Rhyol came back.'

'Why? What happened to the other two?'

'Rhyol had warned them not to fly too far away from

the portal in case it closed before they could get back, but they were so amazed by the strange beauty of the new world they found themselves in that they just kept on flying. Rhyol waited half an hour, and then he decided to go back to Dragonworld on his own. He was only just in time. As soon as he came out of the portal, it closed, and disappeared.'

'Did Graphir and Arkos ever get back to Dragonworld, Menhir?'

'Yes, they did, but not until a long time afterwards. You see, Timothy, Moonbows don't happen at every full moon, and even when they do, not all of them turn blue.

'Rhyol and Kalmandar returned to the stone circle in Dragonworld every twenty-nine days hoping that the portal would open again so that Graphir and Arkos could come home. But the portal didn't open again for six months, and when it did, Rhyol went through it to look for the two missing dragons. He found them easily enough, because they were sitting in the stone circle that he had made in the new world, but what really astonished him was that the two stone dragons were only half as big as they had been when he last saw them.'

'You mean they'd shrunk, Menhir? But how could that have happened?'

'Us dragons have thought about that an awful lot over the years. We have a theory about it. We think that time doesn't work quite the same way in our world as it does in yours, but we don't know why. What we do know is that the longer we stay in your world the

44

smaller we get.

'Because Rhyol and Arkos had been in your world for so long, they weren't big and strong enough to fly back through the portal into Dragonworld against the howling wind.'

'How did Rhyol and Arkos get back then?'

'Rhyol asked them where he could find a long tree branch. They told him about a place in a nearby wood where there were lots of long branches in a pile. Rhyol told them to stay where they were while he quickly flew off and picked up one of the long tree branches with his great, clawed feet.

'When he got back to the stone circle, he told Rhyol to grab hold of one end of the branch, and Arkos to grab hold of the middle. Then he grabbed the other end of the branch so that, with Rhyol leading, the two smaller dragons holding onto the branch behind him, and all three of them using their strength together, they were able to fly against the howling wind, through the portal and back to Dragonworld.'

'So, it was teamwork that got them home!'

'Yes, Timothy, it was. And they had some very exciting news to give to the other dragons. They had discovered creatures that walk upright on two legs, and have arms and hands instead of wings. They called the creatures "humans", so after that, the dragons called your world Humanworld. It was the humans who had cut the tree branches and piled them up in a heap.'

'Menhir, is that the reason why you're so small? Did

you come through the portal and then stay too long?'

'Yes. I came through the portal into Humanworld more than a year ago. There's no way of knowing how long a portal will stay open. Usually, it's about half-an-hour, sometimes much longer. But the last time I came through, the portal closed after just a few minutes.

'I wasn't that worried at first, because since Rhyol, Graphir and Arkos first began to explore your world, dragons have been here many times, although we never stay very long. We found that there are fish in your lakes and rivers and seas that we can eat. But a big stone dragon needs to eat an awful lot of fish every day, and the fish in your world are smaller than the fish in our world, and they are more difficult to catch. So, if we stay too long in your world not only do we get smaller, but because it's more difficult for us to get enough to eat here, we get weaker, too.'

'That's why you're so hungry, then, and it's why you can't fly very far,' said Timothy. 'I expect that being put in a cage and being given bird seed to eat didn't help very much either.'

'No, it didn't. I tried to eat some of it, but it just made me feel ill. I'm no longer big enough, or strong enough, to fly back to where the nearest portal is, and even if I could get there, I wouldn't be able to get through the portal because I'm not strong enough to fly against the howling wind. That's why I need your help.'

'But what can I do, Menhir? I can't make you any bigger or stronger. Where's the nearest portal,

46

anyway?' asked Timothy.

'We made a bargain, remember?' said Menhir. 'Sleep now, Timothy, and I'll tell you the rest of what you need to know tomorrow.'

Chapter 5: The Salmon That Never Was

When Timothy woke up, the summer sun was shining brightly through his open bedroom window. He sat up, stretched, and yawned. Menhir had been curled up on the foot of his bed when he fell asleep, but now there was no sign of him. His alarm clock said it was eight o'clock.

'I wonder where he's got to?' said Timothy out loud.

'I'm underneath your bed,' came the squeaky voice, 'in case your mother comes in.'

'I don't suppose she will, because I usually get myself up. And I make my own bed, and keep my room tidy. You should be safe enough here. You could make her forget that she'd seen me anyway, couldn't you?'

'Taking a memory out of someone's mind takes a lot of effort, Timothy. It takes more effort even than flying does. I managed to do it twice last night, but now all my strength is spent. I need food before I can do it again. For now, I'll just have to hide.'

Timothy realised that he'd only had four hours' sleep. He still felt very tired, but he was hungry too because of all the work he'd done during the night. He got out of bed, and pulled on his bathrobe.

'I'm going down to see if Mum's started doing breakfast, Menhir. I'll be back in a little while.'

'I'd be very grateful if you could find some more food for me, Timothy: I'm still very hungry.'

'I'll do my best, Menhir. I'll try to think of something,' said Timothy.

Saying that reminded him about the two pieces of salmon he'd taken from the fridge during the night, so it was with a trembling heart that he made his way down the stairs.

In the kitchen, his father was eating a slice of toast and marmalade while reading the morning newspaper.

'Hello, Tim,' he said, 'did you manage to sleep all right? We didn't want to wake you up in case you'd had a bad night.'

'No Dad, I didn't sleep very well.'

'That's because it was such a hot, sticky night, I expect,' said his mother from over by the kitchen sink. 'It's always difficult to sleep on nights like that. Now, what would you like for your breakfast, Tim?'

As she turned and reached for the fridge door, Timothy put his hands over his eyes and tried to curl himself up into a ball.

'I've got some bacon to use up, so you could have egg and bacon if you want. Did you enjoy that salmon we had for dinner yesterday?'

'Um … y-yes, Mum. I like salmon.'

'Well, that's good, because fish is the best food you can eat. It has lots of good things in it to make you grow big and strong, and it's good for your brain, too.

It's a pity we used it all up yesterday. I'd meant to get five pieces so that I could make you some fish cakes, but I must have only bought three. Never mind, perhaps I can get some more at the market in town this afternoon.'

Timothy was suddenly very glad that he wasn't standing up, because his knees had gone wobbly.

'Are you all right, Tim?' Asked his father.

'Hmm?'

'You're staring at you mother as though she'd just turned into a monster. And your mouth's open.'

'What? Oh, sorry, Mum. I'm just tired that's all.'

'I was asking if you'd like egg and bacon.'

'Oh … yes please, Mum.'

'You know, you really do look a bit washed-out, old son,' said his father with a smile. 'I think that when you've eaten your breakfast, you'd better go and have a lie-down for a couple of hours. Your mum wants you to go into town with her later on. She's going to pick up your High School uniform, and you'll have to try it on, so you'll need to be wide awake for that.'

It was while Timothy was hungrily scoffing his egg, bacon, toast and marmalade, that the doorbell rang.

'Can you answer that please, Fred?' said Timothy's mother to her husband. His father put down his newspaper and walked along the hallway to the front door. Timothy heard the door open, and enough snatches of the conversation that followed, to realise that it was his neighbour, Mr Fowler, who was at the door. His appetite suddenly vanished as he put down his knife and fork, to wait with a mounting sense of dread as the front door closed.

'Well, there's a turn-up for the book,' his father said as he sat down at the kitchen table.

'Who was it?' asked his mother.

'Our neighbour, Mr Fowler. Apparently, when Tim and David were playing their soft-ball tennis game in the garden yesterday, one of them sent the ball over the garden fence, so Tim went around and asked if he could go and find it. Mr Fowler came to say that he was sorry for the way he snapped at him. He said that he thinks you're a nice lad really, Tim, and that he shouldn't have spoken to you the way he did.'

Timothy could hardly believe his ears. It took a moment or two for it to sink in.

'You didn't say anything about it yesterday, Tim,' said his mother.

Timothy shrugged. 'I didn't want to make a fuss. I just wanted to get the ball back so me and David could finish our game.'

'Who won?' asked his father.

'David did. Three sets to two.'

'Well, there'll be another time, won't there, son? And revenge is best served with a well-aimed overhead slam.'

'I like David,' said Timothy's mother. 'He's always so polite and well-spoken. It's easy to see why the two of them are such good friends.'

'Yes, I agree, Molly,' replied his father, 'David's a nice lad too.'

Timothy's father fished in his pocket, pulled out a handful of change, and laid two one-pound coins on the table.

'This,' he said, sliding one of them across to his son, 'is for being a good boy this week, and helping your mother with the chores. And this,' as he slid the other coin across, 'is for making a good impression on our grumpy old neighbour. Maybe you'll find something you want when you go into town with your mother this afternoon. Now, go up and have a bit more sleep.'

Back up in his bedroom, Timothy found Menhir sitting on his bed. He closed the door and sat down on the edge of the bed. 'You said they'd forget, Menhir, and they did. How did you do that?'

'That's the next thing I've got to explain to you, Timothy, and you must listen carefully, because it's important that you understand.'

'Ok. I'm listening.'

'Good,' said Menhir. 'Now. You see your computer over there on the desk?'

'Yes.'

'Well, in the drawer underneath the computer you've got something called a memory stick. You use it to save photos on, don't you?'

'Yes, Menhir, that's right. But how do you know about things like that?'

'Just listen, Timothy, and everything will become clear, okay?'

'All right.'

'How many photos can that memory stick hold?'

'Um, it depends on the how big the photos are, but probably about a thousand.'

'It's a very small thing, a memory stick, isn't it?'

'Yes, I suppose it is.'

'Well, your brain is an awful lot bigger than a memory stick, and it's a lot better at storing pictures than any memory stick ever was.

'A human brain – and a dragon brain too – can hold millions of pictures. In your head is a picture of everything you've ever seen, or done, or heard, or felt, every single minute of every day since the day you were born. You may not be able to remember them all, but they are there just the same. And you see, Timothy, a dragon can see those pictures when he looks at you in just the same way that you can see the pictures on your memory stick when you plug in into your computer.'

'Can you, Menhir? Can you really?'

'Yes, Timothy, I can. And it's because I can see those pictures that I know who you are.'

Timothy looked at the little dragon with a puzzled frown.

'But I know who I am, Menhir. I'm Timothy Tamworth.'

'No, Timothy, that's a just a name. A name doesn't say anything about what *kind* of person you are; nor does the way you look, or the way you dress, or the way you speak. It doesn't matter what you are called, or what you look like. It doesn't matter what colour your skin is, or where you came from. The only thing that matters is those pictures in your head, because it's your memories that make you who you are.'

'Do they, Menhir? I don't think I completely understand that.'

'That's because you're young, Timothy Tamworth. One day, when you're older, and you've had more experience of life, you'll look back and know that Menhir the stone dragon told you the truth.'

'Okay. But you still haven't told me how you made my mum and Mr Fowler forget.'

'So, tell me what you do if you want to delete one of those photos on your memory stick.'

'I open the photo folder, choose the picture I don't want to keep, and click on "Delete".'

'Right. Dragons can do something very much like that. I look into your head, and I find the memory that I don't want you to keep. But instead of erasing it, I take it out of your head, and put it into mine. Then, I can change it if I want to, and give it back. Or I can delete it. So, what I did with your mother was to take away her memory of buying five pieces of salmon, and replace it with a memory of only buying three pieces. Then, I took away your neighbour's memory of having a strange-looking bird in a cage in his shed, and deleted it.'

'That's amazing, Menhir! Can you do that whenever you want to?'

'Yes, I can. But it's not something a dragon would do just for fun, because it's not really a very good thing to do, and it takes a lot of effort. It's a bit like flying against that howling wind I told you about, so we only do it when we have a very important reason for it. Now then, young Timothy, I believe your father told you to get some sleep, and I think you'd better do that, because you mother wants you to go into town with her later, and when you do that, perhaps you could find a way to get me something to eat.'

Timothy didn't argue because, by that time, he was feeling very tired indeed. He lay down on the bed, and as soon as his head touched the pillow, he fell fast asleep.

Chapter 6: Market Day

Timothy was awoken by his father gently shaking his shoulder.

'Mmm?' He said sleepily.

'Are you feeling better now, Tim?' asked his father.

As Timothy sat up, he suddenly remembered that Menhir was somewhere in the room. 'He's probably under the bed again,' he thought to himself.

'Come on then,' said his father. 'Go and wash your face and brush your hair. Your mum's waiting for you.'

Shortly afterwards, Timothy and his mother were in the bus on their way to the town centre. They went first to the outfitter's shop that sold school uniforms for all the schools in the area. The assistant gave them the pile of things that Mrs Tamworth had ordered, then Timothy and his mother took them into a changing room so that Timothy could try them on.

Timothy looked at himself in the big mirror in the changing room. The uniform looked as though it was a size too large. The navy-blue blazer hung off his shoulders and the grey trouser legs collapsed into folds around his ankles.

'It looks a bit big, Mum,' he said.

'Yes well, that's because you'll grow quite quickly once you start at high school, and if I get you a size

smaller, it'll probably be too small by the time you're halfway through your first year.'

'David's mum will have his uniform altered so it fits him properly.'

'Yes, Tim, I know. But David's parents have more money than we do. They can afford to buy him a new blazer and new trousers every year if they want to, but your dad and me don't have enough money for that. Besides, there's other things you'll need. You'll want at least three shirts, a tie, a jumper, gym shorts and shoes, and I expect you'll be wanting some tennis shoes and a new racquet, too.'

Timothy brightened up at the mention of tennis gear.

'Can I have a new racquet and shoes then, mum?'

'Yes, but I won't be able to afford them if you want your blazer and trousers altered.'

Timothy smiled. 'I don't suppose I'll be the only one whose uniform looks a bit too big at first. These will be fine, mum.'

The outfitter's assistant folded the clothes neatly, put them in a large carrier bag, and gave it to Timothy to carry. After leaving the outfitter's shop they walked to the market square in the town centre.

The fishmonger's stall was set out with lots of plastic trays full of all different kinds of fish. In one of the trays was a great heap of very small silvery-white fish. Timothy looked at them and thought, 'Hey, Menhir likes fish and those small ones look just about the right size for him. He could swallow one of those in one go.'

MACK & ROSE FISHMONGERS

He tugged at his mother's arm. 'What are those little fish called, mum?'

'They're called whitebait. You roll them in flour, then fry them in olive oil until they're golden brown and crispy. Then you sprinkle them with lemon juice, dip them in garlic mayonnaise, and just eat them whole with freshly baked bread, and butter.'

'Whole? You mean with heads and tails and everything?'

'Yes, that's right, Tim. They're very tasty.'

'Mmm. I'd like to try that. Can we get some?'

'All right, if you're sure you'll eat them. All fish is good for you, but oily fish like salmon and whitebait are especially good. I'll get some more salmon too, I think, then I can make those fishcakes for later in the week. And we'll get a nice, fresh French loaf from the baker's stall to eat with the whitebait.'

While they were waiting to be served at the baker's stall, a familiar voice said, 'Hello, Molly. Hello, Tim.'

They turned around to see David and his father, Terry Westfield, standing behind them. David was wearing his school backpack. The handle of a tennis racquet was poking out of the top of it.

'Hello Terry, hello David. Are you doing some shopping too?'

'Yes, we are, Mrs Tamworth. My dad's just got me a new tennis racquet and a pair of tennis shoes.'

'Oh, that's nice for you, David, isn't it? I'm going to get the same for Tim before you start at high school. I'm just going to buy some bread, and then we'll be off home on the bus.'

'No need for that,' said David's father. 'My car's in the car park just down the road. I'll give you a lift. Looks like you've got quite a lot to carry.'

'Thanks, Terry,' said Mrs Tamworth. 'That's very kind of you.'

Timothy thought very quickly. He needed to get food for Menhir, and he suddenly realised that here was his best chance.

'Mum,' he said, 'would you and Mr Thompson mind if David and me stay in the town for a little bit longer? We could come home on the bus later if that's all right.'

'What do you think, Terry?' said Mrs Tamworth to David's father.

'They're both good lads, Molly. They've been into town by themselves before, and they've never got into any trouble, so I don't see why not.'

'You'll need some money for your bus fares home then,' said Timothy's mother.

It's all right, mum. Dad gave me some pocket money, so I've got enough for the bus fare.'

'And I've got my pocket money, too,' said David.

'Typical,' said Mr Thompson with a smile. 'They've got it all planned out, and they're two steps ahead of us, Molly, so we might as well give in and leave them to it. Behave yourselves, boys.'

'And don't be late home,' added Timothy's mother as she and David's father walked off towards the car park.

'Right,' said David after the adults had gone. 'What shall we do, then? Do you want to have a look around the market? We could get ice creams from the van over there.'

'Yes, okay,' replied Timothy,' but there's something I need your help with.'

'What's that?'

'I need to buy some fish from the fishmonger's stall and I need to get them home without my parents knowing about it.'

'Fish? Are you serious? Whatever do you want fish for, Tim?'

'I've got this, this sort of … pet. It's hungry, and it needs fish to eat. Only… my parents don't know I've got it, you see.'

'A pet? Where are you keeping it?'

'In my bedroom.'

'Your bedroom? What is it, a stray cat or something?'

'No, it isn't a cat. It's … it's all a bit difficult to explain. Please, David, help me get the fish home, and I'll show it to you.' Timothy wasn't at all sure if letting David see Menhir was a good idea or not, but he knew that the little dragon was very hungry, and there just didn't seem to be any other way of getting the food to him.

'So, you've got a secret pet?' said David. 'Hey, that's cool. All right, Tim, what do you need me to do?'

'I need you to carry the fish in your backpack. Then, when we get back to my house, we'll go straight up to my bedroom to play a game on my computer, and you keep your backpack on.'

Timothy led David back to the fishmonger's stall. He tried to remember how much his mother had paid for the whitebait that she had bought a little earlier, but he hadn't really been taking all that much notice. 'How many of those whitebait can I have for a pound?' he asked.

'Well, let's see,' said the fishmonger. 'There's about a dozen left, and we'll be closing soon, so you can have all of them for a pound if you want.'

'Ok, I'll take them. Can you double bag them for me please?'

On the way back home in the bus, David kept asking about Timothy's secret pet.

'You say it's not a cat or a dog, Tim. Is it a bird? Some birds eat fish, don't they? And why can't you just tell me?'

'Because you won't believe me. And because I don't want you to be frightened of it.'

'Oh, come on, Tim. I won't be afraid of a pet. Just tell me what it is.'

'It's a dragon.'

David's brow furrowed in puzzlement.

An Iguana

A Gecko

A dragon ? Oh, you mean a reptile: a lizard. It's an iguana, or a gecko, or something like that, yes?'

'No, David. It's a dragon. A real one.'

'Oh, come on. There's no such thing as a dragon. Anyway, if it was a real dragon you wouldn't be able to get it in your bedroom, never mind hide it from your parents, because it'd be way too big.'

'I told you. I said you wouldn't believe me.'

'Well, what do you expect? Do you think I'm really going to believe that you've got a real, live dragon in your bedroom? You're just playing a game, aren't you?'

'No, I'm not playing a game: I'm serious. There's a real dragon in my bedroom. I'm telling you because I don't want you to be frightened when you see it. I don't want you to scream, or shout, or try to run away, because it won't hurt you. It's a friendly dragon, it's in trouble, and it needs my help to get back to where it belongs. It's hungry too, and it's going to be very pleased to get that fish you're carrying. It's a Stone Dragon, and its name's Menhir.'

'Oh, I see. It's a little statue made of cement, or plaster or something that looks like stone.'

'No. David. It's not made of stone. It's called a Stone Dragon because of what it does, not what it's made of. Its name is Menhir, and it can talk.'

'It can *what*?'

Chapter 7: Mindlight

When the boys opened the front door at Timothy's house they called out a greeting to Timothy's mother, who was in the kitchen, as they ran straight up the stairs to his bedroom. At Timothy's bedroom door, they halted.

'Remember what I told you, David,' said Timothy, with his hand on the door knob. 'Don't be scared, and don't shout. He won't hurt you.'

'Oh, come on,' said David with a laugh. 'We're here now. The game's over, so …'

As they walked into the room, Menhir was sitting upright on Timothy's bed with his long tail curled around his feet and his wings folded across his back. David stopped dead in his tracks with his mouth wide open. He pointed at the bed. 'That's … that's a …'

'A dragon, yes. A real one, just like I told you.'

'Hello, David,' said Menhir. 'I'm very pleased to meet you.'

David took a very unsteady step backwards, but Timothy grabbed his arm. 'The first time he spoke to me I tripped over a bucket and fell on the floor. I don't want you falling over because you might hurt yourself, and my mum might come up to see what the noise was about.'

Keeping hold of David's arm, Timothy led him to his

computer desk, telling him to sit down on the swivel chair.

'But … but where did it come from? How did it get into your bedroom?'

'Just sit still for bit and take a few deep breaths while I fill you in on what's been happening for the last couple of days,' said Timothy. 'And you can talk to Menhir, you know, if you want to. He understands what you say and he'll answer your questions. Now, take that backpack off so I can give Menhir his fish while we talk.'

Timothy spent the next half hour sitting on the bed feeding the little dragon with the fish while explaining to his friend all that had happened since he'd been into his next-door neighbour's garden to retrieve that ball.

'Thank you, Timothy,' said Menhir after the boy had popped the last of the whitebait down his throat. 'I feel much better now, and after I've slept for a while, I'll feel much stronger, too.'

'You never told me, Menhir, how you came to be in Mr. Fowler's shed.'

'There's a lot to tell you about that, so bear with me. I've told you that dragons can see the images in your head, Timothy. That's how we tell one dragon from another. The dragon names I've told you about – like Rhyol, Arkos and Kalmandar, are names that humans gave us, but we don't use names among ourselves because we identify other dragons by looking at the pictures in their heads. That's how we talk to each other, too. We don't use spoken words like humans do, we exchange ideas, and news, and experiences by swopping mind pictures with each other. Dragons don't need to be close to each other to be able swop mind pictures. We can do it even when the dragon we want to communicate with is a long way away. That's because a dragon sees another dragon's mind like a searchlight shining out of the top of its head with a bright beam that goes way up into the sky. We call it the mindlight. When we see that mindlight, we know who the other dragon is, and then we can swop mind pictures.'

Sitting on the swivel chair, David had begun to recover from the shock of meeting a real, live dragon for the first time, and he had been listening very carefully to what Menhir was saying.

'Am I right in thinking that the reason you can't tell your dragon friends where you are and what's happened to you is because, once you go through a portal, you can't see their mindlights anymore?'

Menhir nodded his head slowly. 'Yes, David, you're quite right. It's very clever of you to have worked that out so quickly. But I'm not surprised, because you and Timothy both have very bright mindlights.'

'What?' said Timothy with some surprise. 'Do you mean that humans have mindlights too?

'Yes, Timothy, they do. Dragons and humans are the only life-forms that have them, but human mindlights aren't usually as bright as Dragon mindlights. In fact, some of them are quite dim.'

69

'If that's true, Menhir,' said David with a puzzled frown,' why can't I see a light shining out of the top of your head? Does it only show up when it's dark?'

'It's true,' replied the dragon, 'that mindlights show up better at night in your world. But in our world we can see them all the time. Humans, though, can't usually see them at all. But there are rare exceptions, and I think you and Timothy might be able to see them if you practice looking for them. The best place for you to learn to do that would be in Dragonworld.'

Timothy sat up straight, staring at the dragon in astonishment. 'Do you mean we could get to Dragonworld if we wanted to, Menhir?'

'It might be possible, Timothy, but first let me finish explaining how I came to be in that cage in your neighbour's shed, because it's important that you should know.'

Both boys nodded. 'Okay.'

'You have to understand that, when the sun goes down in Dragonworld, there's no light except from the moon and stars. So, it's very easy to see our mindlights then. We usually come through the portal into your world at night, because the moon only shines at night. Moonbow portals only form when it's night in your world and our world at the same time. But your world is different from ours because, here, at night, there's lights everywhere: vehicle lights, streetlights, the lights shining out from your shops, houses, and office blocks. There's so much light that it's difficult to pick out dragon mindlights among all the other lights.

'The other dragons won't give up looking for me, you see. They'll understand where I've gone. So, every time a moonbow portal opens, one or two of them will come through and fly around looking for my mindlight. But they can't stay for very long, or fly very far from the portal, in case they get trapped here too.'

'And with all the lights in our world,' put in Timothy, 'they might not see your mindlight anyway, even if you weren't all that far away from them.'

'Exactly so,' said Menhir. 'When I began to get really worried, I circled round and round, high up in the sky, further and further from where the portal I'd come through had formed. I was looking for dragon mindlights; thinking that, maybe, another dragon might have come through from a different portal somewhere else in your world, trying to find me.

'One night, when I'd been searching for about six months, and was starting to think that I'd never get home again, I saw *your* mindlight far away in the distance to the south, Timothy, and your mind-pictures told me that you were someone who wouldn't run away screaming when you saw me because your sense of curiosity is stronger than your fear. So, I began to fly south.'

'But you said you've been in this world for a year, Menhir. Did it really take you another six months to get from where the portal was to my neighbour's garden?'

'Yes, because when I flew away from the lake after the first six months, I was already only half as big as I had been before I left Dragonworld. I could only fly at night because, if I flew during the day, humans would see me. They would probably have tried to capture me, or, if they were really frightened, they might have tried to kill me.'

'But couldn't you make them forget they'd seen you?'

'If I flew during daylight, I would have had to make humans forget that they'd seen me dozens of times every day. I've told you that it takes a lot of mental effort to do that, and no dragon has the strength to keep on doing it day after day after day. Once I moved away from the lake where the portal formed I couldn't find any more fish to eat. With every day that passed, I grew smaller and smaller, and more and more weak from hunger. I became so weak that I couldn't fly high enough to see where I needed to go. I lost my way; I couldn't see the lake any more where I'd started out from, and I couldn't be sure that I was going in the right direction.

 'When I became too weak to fly at all, I walked. I found places to hide up in during the day, and I walked at night, scrambling through hedges and over fences, hoping against hope that I'd find you, Timothy. And then, one day when I was so weak that I couldn't walk any more, your neighbour found me lying in his garden. He thought I was some sort of bird, so he picked me up and put me in a cage.

'I'd only been in the cage a couple of days when I heard you and your friend playing on the other side of the fence. I knew it was you, of course, because I

72

could see your mind pictures. The rest of it you already know.'

'Then, if I hadn't mis-hit the ball and sent it over the fence,' said David,' Tim wouldn't have gone to look for it, and you'd still be in that cage.'

'That's right David. And I probably wouldn't have survived for much longer. So, the truth is, I owe you and Timothy my life.'

Chapter 8: Circles and Time

The boys looked at each other, and then at the dragon.

'Ok, Menhir,' said Timothy,' I think we understand how, and why, you got here. Now you need to tell us how to help you get home, even if we don't quite understand where Dragonworld is.'

'To help me get home, you have to take me to a stone circle. It has to be a stone circle that was originally made by dragons, because that's where portals form.'

'You're saying that not all stone circles were made by dragons?'

'Correct, Timothy. As I've told you, it was dragons, not humans, who first began to make stone circles. They did it to mark the places where portals form. But later, humans began to copy the circles because they thought stone circles were magical.'

'Which stone circle do you need to get to?'

'I wish I could tell you, but I'm no longer certain. I flew south to get here, so it must be to the north, but all I can remember is that it was near a big lake where I caught a lot of fish.'

'There's a famous stone circle not far from here,' said David.

'Yes, I know. You humans call it Stonehenge. It's in a place that you call Salisbury Plain. But, for a portal to form, you need to have lots of water nearby. It has to be near a large lake, or a waterfall, or be close to the sea. There's no lake on Salisbury plain, so dragons didn't build that one.'

'I know something we could try,' said David. 'Let's look online and find out where there are stone circles with lakes near them.'

Timothy switched on his computer, and when it had loaded up, he entered "stone circles near lakes" in the search engine. After a few moments a list appeared on the screen. Timothy brought up a map on the screen that showed where all the stone circles are.

'There's a stone circle at a place called Castlerigg,' he said. 'It's in the Lake District. Look, there's lots of lakes in that area. Do you think that might be the one, Menhir?'

'I don't know, Timothy,' said the dragon. 'Can your computer show me what it looks like?'

He jumped off the bed, flapped his wings, and landed on the back of Timothy's swivel chair so that he could look over the boy's shoulder at the computer screen.

'Try looking at it on Google Street View,' suggested David.

Timothy tried to do that, but he couldn't find a spot on a nearby road that gave a clear, close-up view of the stone circle.

'Wait a minute, I'll put "Castlerigg" in the search engine and get a proper photo of it.'

When the photo came up on the screen Menhir said, 'Yes, that's it. That's the stone circle where the portal forms. I'm sure of it. I remember the shape of that big mountain that stands behind it. And look, you can see that the stones of the circle are all different shapes and sizes. That's a sure sign that it was dragons who made it. The first dragon to come through the portal there probably just put down four or five great rocks that he found lying about, and then other dragons who used the portal later, would have added a few more rocks.'

'Those stones look awfully big,' said Timothy,

looking closely at the photograph. 'Could a stone dragon lift rocks as big as that, Menhir?'

'Oh yes, quite easily. Looking at me as I am now, you have no idea how big a fully-grown stone dragon is. If you took out all the floors and internal walls from this house, you might just about squeeze one into it. Look at my feet. They have four toes; three pointing forwards and one pointing back. The toes of a stone dragon are each about a metre long, and they have huge, curved claws on the ends of them. Like mine, but much bigger.'

Timothy, with his mouth wide open, turned his head around to look at Menhir perched on the back of his chair. He was trying to think of something to say, but David was already speaking.

'If that's the right circle,' said David, 'then there must be a lake nearby. In Street View I saw a river near the circle, but it didn't look like very big one. That might not be enough water to cause a moonbow. Go back to

Google Maps and zoom out a bit.' Timothy turned back to the computer to do as David had asked him.

'There, look, down to the south-west of the circle. There's a big lake there. Zoom in on it.'

'Yes, I see it,' said Timothy. 'It's called Derwentwater. I'll try to find a spot on the road that runs along by it to see where we can get a clear view of the lake.'

He picked up the little yellow pegman and dropped him onto the road near the lake. After a few minutes of working his way along the road, he came to a spot free of trees where there was a good view of the lake and the hills beyond it.

'What do you think, Menhir?'

'What I think, Timothy Tamworth,' replied the dragon, 'is that's the lake where I caught all those fish. And I think that you and your friend are very clever young humans.'

After a few moments silence, David asked, 'How far away is Castlerigg?'

Using Google maps, Timothy put a marker on his house and then another on the stone circle. The program immediately showed them the route from the house to the circle, and how many miles away it was.

'Let's see: The two nearest towns to the Castlerigg stone circle are Keswick and Penrith. Keswick is closest, and it's right beside Derwentwater. It's two hundred and eighty-five miles to Keswick from here. If we went by road it'd take four-and-a-half hours.'

'How on earth are we going to get there, then?' asked David. 'Do you think maybe it'd be a good idea to tell your parents, or mine, about Menhir and ask them to help?'

'No, we aren't going to tell anyone, because if we do, they'll try to catch Menhir and put him in a cage. Then the police or the RSPCA would come and take him away. We would never see him again, and he would never get back to Dragonworld. I'm not having that, David. I promised Menhir I'd help him to get home and I'm going to do it no matter how far away the portal is.'

'Ok, Tim, take it easy: I'm with you on this. Whatever we need to do, we're going to do it together. We have to get Menhir to Castlerigg. We can't walk there because it's too far, and we'd have to be away for days on end if we did that. We'd have our parents and the police looking for us, so we'd never make it on foot even if we tried. And we can't go by car, either.'

'There's only one way, David. We have to go by train.' He pointed to the computer screen. 'Look, Google Maps shows the route of the railway going north. We could get on a train at Oxford. The nearest railway station to Castlerigg is at Penrith.'

'Ok, so how much would the tickets cost?' asked David. 'I've got about ten pounds in my piggy bank at home.'

'I think I've got about five pounds,' replied Timothy as he logged off from Google Earth, and logged on to the National Rail website.

Very quickly, he realised that the tickets would cost far more money than they could ever get their hands on. He turned to Menhir.

'Menhir, the only way we can get to you Castlerigg is on the train, but the tickets would cost sixty pounds each. There's no way we could get enough money to buy them.'

'Explain to me about money and tickets,' said the dragon.

The boys spent the next ten minutes trying to explain to Menhir about money and buying things.

'So let's see if I've got this right,' said the dragon. 'You go to the train station and give someone money. That person gives you a ticket to show that you've paid your fare. I am right so far?'

The boys nodded.

'Then, when you've got the ticket, you use it to get past a barrier so you can get on the train, yes?'

'Yes, that's right.'

'While you're on the train, someone called an inspector comes along and asks to see your ticket. And then, when you get off the train, you use the ticket to get past the barrier and leave the station.'

'Yes, Menhir, that's right.'

'Well, you don't have worry about tickets because you won't need them. I can help with that. As far as these barrier things are concerned, I might be able to find a way for you to get past them, but since neither of you has a clear picture of how they work in your heads, you will have to wait until I've seen them until I can be sure about it.'

'Okay,' said Timothy, 'we'll go with that. Listen, David, I've told you that dragons don't lie, so if Menhir says he can do something you can be sure he's telling the truth.'

'On that subject, Timothy,' said the dragon,' I want to try a little experiment with you.'

'What do you mean … experiment? What sort of experiment?'

'I'm going to send you a mind picture. I want you to tell me what you see in your mind's eye.'

'Hey, that sounds cool. Okay, go ahead.'

A moment later, Timothy eyes opened as wide as his jaw dropped. The a huge and delighted grin spread across his face.

'I can see your world, Menhir! I can see Dragonworld! There's lots of islands in a huge sea, and a few, I think it was three of those islands, had volcanoes on them!'

'Exactly so. I was right about you, Timothy, you have a very bright mindlight and a brain as receptive as a dragon's. In all my life I have only ever known one other human like you. As I've told you, that's how dragons talk to each other, and that's why we can't lie. You can only lie if you use words. But when you exchange mind pictures it's not possible to lie.'

'How old *are* you, Menhir?' asked David.

'That's not easy to work out. Let me see if I can

explain. You probably know that a year is the time it takes for the Earth to complete one orbit around the Sun, yes?'

'Yes,' replied David. 'We've done that in our science class at school.'

'And you probably also know that a day is the length of time it takes for the Earth to spin once around its own axis?'

'Yes, we know that, too.'

'Well now, the fact is that the Earth is moving very slowly away from the Sun. It's only moving by a tiny amount each year, but over a very long period of time, as the Earth gets farther away from the Sun, it takes longer and longer for the Earth to complete its journey around the Sun, because it has further to travel, and that in turn, means that the years are getting longer.'

'Are they really, Menhir?'

'Yes, they are. Not only that, but the speed at which the Earth rotates around its own axis is slowing down, which means that the days are getting longer too.'

'Wow, I never knew that,' said Timothy.

'Hey, that's not fair,' said David. 'It means that, every year, we're spending longer and longer at school.'

'Yes,' replied Timothy, 'but it also means that evenings and weekends are longer too, so we're not losing any of our leisure time either. Right, Menhir?'

'Exactly so, Timothy. But to answer your question,

David, I suppose that in your Humanworld years I'm about a hundred and thirty.'

The boys were quiet for few moments as they tried to take in what the dragon had told them.

'But … but, wait a minute, Menhir,' said Timothy. 'You told me yesterday that it was ancient humans who gave you your name way back when stone circles were first being built. It says, in one of my history books that stone circles were first built in Humanworld five or six thousand years ago. So how could you have been in Humanworld all that time ago if you're only a hundred and thirty years old?'

'Ah, now that's something I was going to tell you about later. I've already given your young minds quite a lot to take on board, and I didn't want to confuse you. But since you ask, the reason is this:

'When Portals form in Dragonworld they always come out in the same places in Humanworld. So, we always know *where* each portal leads to. What we don't know, is *when* they will lead to until we go through them, because they don't always lead to the same *time*. For example, I've been to your world tens of millions of years ago when there weren't any humans on the Earth at all. I've been here two thousand years ago when the Romans occupied your land, and I've been here six thousand years ago when humans first began to copy our stone circles.'

Chapter 9: Camping Out.

While the boys were quietly thinking that over, Timothy's mother called up the stairs.

'Timothy, would David like to stay for dinner?'

Timothy's head whipped around. He was nodding quickly, while mouthing, 'Say yes! Say yes!'

David gave him a puzzled look as he moved across the room and opened the door, but he called out, 'Yes, please, Mrs Tamworth, I'd like to stay for dinner. Can I use your phone to let my parents know?'

'Yes, David, of course you can. You know where it is. We're going to have the whitebait I bought this morning, and then cheesecake with ice-cream for pudding.'

'Sounds great, Mrs Tamworth. Thank you.'

Timothy sat staring at the computer screen, his mind racing, thinking about how they would get to Castlerigg, and when they would have to go.

'Menhir, there was a bright moon last night when I got you out of that cage. It was almost full, but not quite. There was just a little bit of it missing. Does that mean there's going to be a full moon tonight?'

'The full moon will be tomorrow night,' answered the dragon.

'If a portal's going to open, that's when it will happen, isn't it?'

'Yes, provided there's lot of moisture in the air. It has to be a clear night with no clouds, and there has to be enough moisture to cause a moonbow.'

'And you say that there's only a full moon every four weeks?'

'It's every four weeks in Dragonworld, that's once every twenty-eight days. But in your world, it happens once every twenty-nine-and-a half days.'

'Does it?' asked David. 'Why is that, Menhir?

'We don't really know. But maybe one day, one of you clever humans will work it out for us.'

'Okay. We can't hide you and feed you for a whole month, Menhir, 'said Timothy, 'so we need to act quickly. I think I know what we have to do. When you phone your parents, David, ask them if you can stay for dinner and then sleep over for the night.'

'Hey, that'll be fun, Tim. Will your parents let me do that?'

'We'll talk to them about it when we have dinner, but I think they'll be okay with it.'

'Have you got a plan, then?'

'Yes, listen. There'll be a full moon tomorrow night, and we have to be at Castlerigg when it happens, so that means we have to start out tonight.'

'Why tonight? It won't take all that time to get to the stone circle, will it?'

'No it won't, but we can't just walk out of here with Menhir during the day. My parents will want to know where we're going, and they'll stop us doing it if they know why. What we're going to do is camp out on the lawn. So, you need to go home and get your sleeping bag. You'll need your backpack too, but that's already here, and a fleece hoody. I know you've got one because I've seen you wearing it.'

'We'll need a tent if we're going to camp out.'

'We've got one. It's one of those pop-up tents. You only have to push the poles into the sides and it's done. It's kept up in the roof space. My dad'll get it down for us if I ask him to. It's only a small tent, but it's big enough for us, and it'll do because we won't actually be in it for very long anyway.'

'So we wait until everyone's asleep, and then we go. Is that it?'

'That's the idea, yes.'

'Okay, but how are we going to get to Oxford station?'

'We'll walk. It'll take about an hour, I think, but we can sleep once we get on the train.'

'How are we going to get Menhir there? The people at the station are going to see him if he walks, and he's too big and heavy to go in a backpack.'

'My mum's got one of those two-wheeled shopping trolleys. She uses it sometimes when she goes to the supermarket. We'll borrow it and put him in that. It's kept in the lobby by the back door, and that's where my hoody's hung up, too. We can get them easily when we leave because Mum and Dad won't lock the back door while we're out in the tent, in case we need to come in.

'Menhir might have to curl up a bit in the trolley, but I think he'll fit. I can put my sleeping bag in the bottom so's he'll have something comfy to sit on, and we'll leave the zipper slightly open so he can breathe.'

'Looks like you've got it all worked out, dragon brain.'

Timothy grinned as his face flushed. 'Don't start calling me that, David, or I'll thump you one.'

David was laughing as he left the room to go downstairs and phone his parents.

While he was gone, Timothy went over the journey details with Menhir.

'According to Google, Menhir, the total journey time from Oxford to Penrith by train is five hours and twenty minutes. The first part of the journey is Oxford to Manchester. There's a train that leaves at six-thirty in the morning. It takes about three hours to get to Manchester. Then we have to wait an hour for the train from there to Penrith. That second part of the journey takes an hour and a half. So, if we get the six-thirty train from Oxford tomorrow morning, we should be at Penrith by midday. Then, I guess we'll have to hope we can catch a bus from there to Castlerigg. There's bound to be a bus stop near the stone circle, because a lot of people go there to see it.'

He was looking at those places on the map on his

computer screen as he spoke, while Menhir, still perched on the back of Timothy's chair, followed his pointing finger. 'Let's see. The main road from Penrith to Keswick is called the A66. There's certain to be a bus going along that way. But the stone circle is some way to the south of the main road. Still, we can walk that bit if we have to. Do you think you'd be okay in a shopping trolley?'

'It seems to me that my fate is entirely in your hands, Timothy,' said the dragon. 'So, if I have to travel in a shopping trolley to get home, then I will. But I have to say that, even though you're a very young human, I

don't think I could have found a better pair of hands.'

David came back into the bedroom and sat down on the bed.

'My dad says okay to staying for dinner, and sleeping over. He offered to bring my sleeping bag, and some other stuff, round in the car, but I said no, I'd come and get them after dinner.'

'Hey, that's great,' said Timothy. 'But why not let your dad bring the stuff?'

'Well, if I don't go home, I won't be able to get the

money out of my piggy bank, and it seems to me that we're going to need it because, if we're going to be away for a couple of days, we'll need to buy something to eat.'

'Good thinking, Batman,' replied Timothy. 'My mind's been so full of the details of the journey that I hadn't even thought about food. We'll need to get some more food for Menhir too, if we can. By the looks of it, we'll have about fifteen pounds between us. There'll be some bus fares to pay for, so we'll just have to be very careful how we spend the rest of it.'

After Timothy had explained to David what he'd worked out for the journey to Castlerigg, Timothy's mother called up that dinner was almost ready. While Menhir curled up safely under the bed, the boys washed their hands in the bathroom and went downstairs.

The whitebait, fried crisp and golden, turned out to be every bit as tasty as Mrs Tamworth had said it would be. Even the tails were good, melting in the mouth like salty potato crisps. But no one seemed to want to eat the heads. Without discussing the matter, each of the four diners carefully cut them off, laying them aside before dipping the fishy bodies in the little dishes of garlic mayonnaise that accompanied each plate.

When the first course was finished, and Timothy's mum got up to collect the used crockery, Timothy said, 'I'll clear the table mum, while you get the cheesecake.'

He took a couple of sheets of kitchen tissue from the

roll on the worktop, carefully collected the fish heads from each plate into the tissue, then went out to the back lobby as though to throw them into the waste bin there. Instead, and without anybody seeing, he quickly dropped the tissue-wrapped heads into his mother's shopping trolley and zipped the top closed. Then he went back to clear away the plates, dishes and cutlery, placing them on the worktop by the dishwasher. David grinned at him as he sat down again.

While the slices of lemon cheesecake were being served, Timothy asked, 'Dad, would it be okay for David to stay and sleep over for the night?'

Mr Tamworth looked up at his wife, who nodded her agreement.

'Yes, Tim. David would be welcome to stay overnight if he wants to.'

'It's going to be another hot, sticky night. So I wondered if it'd be all right for me and David to camp out on the lawn.'

'What do you think, Molly?' asked Timothy's father.

'Well, I suppose it's okay,' replied Timothy's mother, 'as long as David asks his parents first.'

'I've already done that, Mrs Tamworth,' said David. 'I asked my dad when I phoned about dinner. He said it would be okay.'

'You'll be wanting the tent, then, I expect,' said Mr Tamworth. 'I'll go up and get it out of the roof for you.'

'Thanks, dad,' said Timothy, 'that'd be great.'

'You'll need sweaters in case it gets chilly during the night,' said Mrs Tamworth.

'I'm going home after dinner to get my sleeping bag, Mrs Tamworth,' said David. 'I'll bring a hoodie top back, too.'

When the boys had finished eating, and David had thanked Timothy's parents for the meal, they went back up to Timothy's bedroom.

'I think I'll be a bit worried about them sleeping outdoors, Fred.'

'Oh, they'll be fine Molly. The side gate'll be bolted, and we'll leave the back door unlocked in case they need to come in. It's going to be a warm night, like Tim said. They're good, sensible lads, both of them. They won't get themselves into any trouble, and it'll be an adventure for them.'

On his way up into the roof to get the tent, Timothy's dad poked his head around the bedroom door. Menhir, who had heard him coming, had disappeared under the bed.

'What are you two going to do to amuse yourselves in the tent?'

'We're going to pretend we're explorers on an expedition in the jungle,' said Timothy with a grin.

'Keep clear of the swamps, then,' replied his father trying his best not to grin back. 'There might be crocodiles in them.'

Chapter 10: Tickets and Trains

As the sun began to set that evening, and David had returned from his walk home and back, bringing his sleeping bag and other things, the boys set to work erecting the tent and pegging it down. It was, as Timothy had said, very easy to do. Just as they were putting their sleeping bags in place, Timothy's father came out into the garden carrying a plastic ice cream box.

'Hey, Livingstone,' he said, 'here's a few supplies for the expedition.'

Timothy recognised the name of the famous explorer, and grinned as he took the box from his dad. Inside it were two small packets of cheesy biscuits, two bags of jelly sweets, and a bar of chocolate.

Inside the tent, when Timothy's father had gone, David looked at the box of goodies. 'Mmm,' he said, 'these look tasty.'

'That's breakfast, that is,' said Timothy. 'We can have a few jellies tonight, but we mustn't eat any more of it until we get to the station. I've already got breakfast for Menhir.'

'Fish heads, right?' replied David as he unpacked his backpack. 'I thought you'd find a way to keep them. Where are they?'

'In my mum's shopping trolley.'

David laughed. 'Nice one, Tim. I've brought my hoody, a torch, two drinker bottles of water, and all the money from my piggy bank. I've got my tablet computer, too. It's got Walkway on it, so we can use it to find our way to the station tomorrow morning.'

'What's Walkway?'

'It's a map program that always shows you where you are, how to get to where you want to go, and how far away it is. It's made for walkers. It shows all the road names and things.'

'Hey, that's cool. It'll save us getting lost.'

'That's what I thought, too. It should be quite easy getting to Oxford station, Tim. All we have to do is follow Cumnore Hill Road, then Westway. That'll take us under the A34. Then there's three river bridges to cross in Botley Road. The last one's called Osney Bridge. After that, the road goes under the railway, and then the station is on the left-hand side of the road. Like you said, it should take us about an hour to walk there.' He tapped the tablet with a finger. 'I looked it all up on here before I left home.'

'Great work, David. That tablet's going to come in handy when we get to Penrith. I think we've got everything we need, so we'd better try to get some sleep now.'

They didn't undress because they wanted to be ready to go as soon as they woke up. It was a warm night, so they didn't get into the sleeping bags, but simply lay down on top of them. As they settled down, they heard a flapping noise outside the tent. Timothy got up to peer through the tent opening.

'Oh, it's you, Menhir,' he said. 'Do you want to come in the tent with us?'

'No,' replied the dragon, 'I'll be okay out here in the garden. I'll wake you when it's time to leave.'

Timothy had brought his battery alarm clock down from his bedroom. He had intended to set the alarm for five o'clock, but he was happy to leave it to Menhir to decide when they should go, so he didn't switch the alarm on.

Timothy woke up when the dragon jumped on this legs. 'It's time, Timothy,' he said. David woke up too. Both of them rubbed their eyes and shivered a little, because the air was quite cool. David pulled his hoody on, and put the plastic box of treats in his backpack.

Outside the tent it was still dark, but there was just a small tinge of light showing on the eastern horizon. Timothy looked at his alarm clock. It said five o'clock in the morning. He rolled up his sleeping bag and tucked it under his arm.

They crept up to the back door. Timothy opened it very quietly, took his hoody from its peg, pulled it on, and carefully lifted the shopping trolley over the doorstep. Then he closed the door, folded his sleeping bag into the bottom of the trolley, laying it flat on the ground so that Menhir could crawl into it.

'Hold on tight, Menhir,' he whispered,' I'm going to stand the trolley up.'

At the garden gate, they paused while David slowly

eased the top and bottom bolts back, and pulled it open. When he had closed it and they set off along the darkened street towards Cumnore Hill, their long journey had begun.

A couple of cars passed along the main road with their headlights on. David said, 'Don't look at them. Just keep your eyes down on the path ahead.'

The sky grew gradually lighter as they walked, Timothy pulling the trolley, and David with his backpack, the tablet computer in one hand. The night was still and quiet, just as it had been the night before. The only noise they could hear, apart from their feet clumping as they walked, was the sound of fish heads being scrunched inside the trolley bag.

'Is your breakfast okay for you, Menhir?' asked Timothy.

'Not as good as fresh fish,' came the muffled reply,' but a lot better than bird seed.'

When they reached the junction with Eynsham Road, David checked their route on his tablet.

'We're in Westway,' he said. 'If we keep going straight on along the dual carriageway, we'll come to the underpass that goes under the A34. After the underpass we'll be in Botley Road. It's twenty past five on the 26th of August, and we're making good time.'

'Oh, so your tablet tells you the time and the date, too?'

'Yeah. All computers do that. So does your desktop.'

They walked along Westway until it became Botley Road, then crossed the three river bridges. Finally, they passed under the railway bridge, and turned left into the station car park, which was also a busy bus station. A double-decker pulled up as another one drew away.

On the station concourse, they stopped and looked around. 'What do we do now, Tim? We can't go and buy tickets because we haven't got enough money. How are going to get through those barriers?'

There didn't seem to be any station staff about, but there were some other people who had just got off the bus and were now putting their tickets into the slots in the barrier machines so that the barriers would open to let them through.

'Wait a minute, David. I'm getting some images from Menhir. Ah, now I see how we can do it. Watch me, then copy what I do.'

Quickly, Timothy got right behind a smartly dressed man carrying a briefcase. When the man put his ticket in the slot, it popped out of another slot on top of the machine. As the man grabbed his ticket, the barrier opened, and the man walked forward with Timothy following so closely behind him that he was through before the barrier could close again.

He looked back at his friend and saw that he was standing right behind a woman pulling a wheelie suitcase. When the barrier opened, he followed her quickly through it. No-one seemed to take any notice of the boys at all.

They looked at the overhead indicator board, and saw that the six-thirty train to Manchester would be leaving from platform two.

'We're on the right platform' said David. 'All we have to do now is wait. It's ten minutes past six. We've done well so far.'

While they waited for the train to arrive, they sat down on a bench to eat their bags of cheesy biscuits.

'Would you like a biscuit, Menhir?' asked Timothy.

'No thanks,' came the reply from inside the trolley bag. 'But if you could get some fish when we reach Manchester I'd be very grateful.'

Timothy couldn't think of how they were going to manage that, but he said, 'I'll try to, Menhir.'

The train arrived, the doors opened, and they stepped on board. There were only a few people on it, the nearest being several seats away from where they stood. They spotted seats for two just in front of a luggage rack.

'We'll sit here,' said Timothy, 'so's no one can sit right behind us.' They squeezed the trolley in between them as the train pulled away from Oxford station.

For the first half-an-hour, the boys sat looking out of the window, watching the changing landscape rushing by. They ate the last of the jelly sweets, but agreed to save the chocolate bar for later in the day. Then, because they had had to get up so early, they both began to feel sleepy.

David was the first to nod off.

Chapter 11: Dreams and Dog Food

He was standing in what seemed to be a very large meadow, perhaps as much as a mile across. The ground beneath the grass under his feet looked white and chalky. Gazing slowly around, he could see that the meadow was completely surround by trees. He had a feeling that, beyond those trees, although he couldn't see it, lay a vast, almost endless, forest.

Away over to his left, what looked like a small herd of deer were grazing along the tree-line at the edge of the forest. Closer to him, a few sheep and goats wandered, nibbling the grass. He couldn't see any fences.

He didn't know where he was, or how he came to be there. He was puzzled, but not frightened. The meadow, the trees and the animals all seemed to be perfectly normal. He felt, in an odd sort of way, that he belonged there; that he was *meant* to be there, and that there was nothing in this place to be scared of. He didn't wonder where David had got to because he knew, somehow, that his friend wouldn't be there.

When he turned to look across the meadow to his right, he was astonished. There, over to one side of the meadow, a group of people were working around a circle of great standing stones. These stones were not like the odd-shaped, odd-sized stones that he'd seen in the photo of Castlerigg. Although some of the great stones were wider than others, they were all roughly similar in shape, with four sides and a flat top. He guessed that they must be more than ten feet tall.

As he walked closer, he could see that there were lots of other great stones lying on the ground, and that the people were working on some of them with stone hammers, shaping and smoothing the sides. He stopped about fifty metres away from the people to stand watching them.

He was suddenly aware of man standing beside him.

A long, green cloak covered his back and shoulders. His bushy iron-grey hair and beard framed a face tanned by sunshine, and weathered by age. Around his neck was a necklace of brightly coloured beads, with what looked like a round, golden medallion where the necklace rested against the middle of his chest. In his hand was a long, ornately carved, wooden staff.

'Greetings, Timothy Brightmind,' he said. 'Welcome to this place.'

'Who are you?'

'I am called Kannith. My people call me "Dragon Master", but you and I both know that no human could ever master dragons.'

'You know about dragons, then?'

'Yes, Timothy, of course. That's why you're here.'

'Is it? Where am I, then?'

'I think you know.'

Timothy looked around again, at the great circle of standing stones, at the chalky ground beneath the grass, and the trees that surrounded the meadow.

'Is this Stonehenge?'

'Well, it's a Henge, and it's made of stone. So I suppose that would be a good name for it, yes.'

'And I'm here because I know about dragons?'

'You're here because Longstone sent you, Timothy Brightmind. He wants you to see something.'

'Longstone? Do you mean Menhir?'

'Yes, that's right. We call him Longstone because he's very good at finding the long stones we need to build the Henge. You'll see him in a moment.'

Kannith raised his staff and pointed it towards the sky. 'Look, here he comes.'

As he raised the staff, the people working on the stones dropped their tools and began moving quickly towards the trees.

'Where are they all going?' asked Timothy.

'They are afraid of Longstone. You and I know that no dragon would ever harm a human, but they don't.'

'Why don't you just tell them, then?'

'Because it suits my purpose not to. There are many things you don't yet understand, Timothy Brightmind, but you will, in time. As you grow older you will learn much about people, and about dragons.

Dragons themselves have told me so, and dragons don't lie.'

As Kannith finished speaking, a massive dragon came spiralling down out of the sky. It was so big that just one of its wings would have covered the whole of Timothy's garden. If it had picked up a family-sized car in each of its huge, taloned feet it could have used them like roller skates.

The dragon descended onto one of the stones that the people had been working on, and then rose up again, hovering over the circle with the great, smoothed stone gripped horizontally in its mighty talons. Then it came down slowly, slowly, to place the stone very carefully across the tops of two of the upright standing stones.

Timothy gasped, and then a delighted smile broke out across his face. 'So *that's* how they did it,' he said.

'How who did what?'

David's voice seemed to be coming from the other end of a tunnel. The dream faded as Timothy found himself back on the train.

'Come on sleepy head, wake up. We'll have to get off in a minute. We're almost at Manchester.'

'David, did anyone ask to see our tickets while I was asleep?'

'When the ticket inspector walked past us, he just nodded at me and smiled. Menhir said that he'd put a picture in the inspector's head of him checking our tickets, so he thought he'd already done it. It's pretty cool having a dragon for a friend, isn't it?'

'You sent me that dream, too, didn't you Menhir?' said Timothy to the trolley.

'Did you like it?' replied the dragon.

'Yes, very much. But there's still a lot I don't understand.'

'Were you frightened by it?'

'No, I wasn't. I found it very interesting.'

'That's good, then. Interest comes first, understanding comes later.'

'What's all this about a dream, then, Tim?'

'I'll tell you while we're waiting for our connection to Penrith.'

The train was slowing down. Out of the window they could see the end of the platform approaching, so they got up and began moving towards the doors.

As the boys walked down the long platform, their stomachs started to rumble. They had shared the bar of chocolate on the train from Oxford, but they hadn't had a proper meal since dinner on the day before.

'One of the girls in our class at school came here last year,' said David. 'I remember her telling me about it. There's a whacking great shopping mall here somewhere. It's part of the station complex.'

'Oh great!' said Timothy. 'We'll be able find somewhere to get something to eat. I expect Menhir's hungry too.'

Ahead of them they could see the ticket barriers.

'We don't have to go through the barriers to get to the platform where the Penrith train goes from,' said David, 'but I think we'll have to go through them to get to the shops.'

When they were closer to the barriers, they could see that there was some sort of problem with them. The entrances had been sealed off with blue and white striped tape. To the left of where the automatic ticket barriers stood, a temporary barrier, like a sort of moveable fence, had been set up. The passengers ahead of them were moving slowly through a gap in that fence as two of the station staff checked their tickets.

'Let's wait a minute, and let the crowd die down a bit,' said Timothy. 'Try to look as though we're waiting for our parents or something.'

They turned around to stand looking back down the platform, craning their necks as though expecting to see someone they knew.

After a few minutes they turned around again, to find that the crowd of passengers had gone. The two men who had been checking tickets had moved, and were now looking away from the gap in the fence.

'Come on,' said Timothy, 'now's our chance. Walk quickly, but don't run.'

They slipped through the gap in the fence while the two ticket inspectors still looked the other way. Once they were out on the concourse, they checked the indicator board, noting which platform they needed to go to later, then walked quickly away towards the station entrance, following the signs that pointed to the shopping mall.

It was, indeed, a very big mall. They soon noticed a shop selling food. 'We'll come back here and get ourselves a burger and coffee,' said Timothy. 'We can afford that, because we haven't spent any of our money yet. But let's get something for Menhir first.'

In a nearby mini-supermarket, they walked along the aisles looking for something that Menhir might like. Timothy spotted some foil trays of dog food. 'Here, this might be all right, David. The trays have strip tops that you just pull off. And look, this one says it's got salmon in it.'

'It's a sealed tray,' said David,' so the food inside should be fresh. Would that be okay, Menhir?'

'I'm hungry enough to eat rats,' replied the dragon from inside the trolley bag. 'So dog food with salmon in it sounds pretty good to me.'

'We'll get two of those trays, then,' said Timothy. 'Menhir can have one when we're back in the station, and other one later this afternoon.' They took the trays to the check-out and paid for them. David put them in his backpack.

Outside the mini supermarket, Timothy stopped to look at the change that the check-out operator had given him.

'That's strange,' he said as he counted the money in his hand. 'The check-out girl's given me back exactly the same money as I gave to her.'

They looked at each other, and then down at the

trolley.

'I'm just doing my bit to help,' said the squeaky voice.

Back at the food shop, when David went in to buy the burgers and coffees, the same thing happened again.

They left the shopping mall and returned to the station entrance. When they got to the temporary barrier there was no one around at all. There weren't any travellers waiting by the gap, and there didn't seem to be any station staff around either. They slipped through, and found a bench seat where they could sit down to eat their burgers and drink their coffee. Timothy opened a tray of dog food to place it inside the trolley bag so that Menhir could eat it without being seen.

'I feel bad about not paying for things. It seems dishonest,' he said.

'Well, I wouldn't worry about that too much,' replied David. 'Once Menhir's gone back through the portal, we won't have him to help us anymore. We've still got to get back home somehow, haven't we? And it won't just be a question of buying food, will it? We can't buy train tickets with just fifteen pounds, even if we've still got all of it.'

Up until that moment, Timothy had been feeling very pleased with the way things had gone. He'd been so concerned with just getting Menhir to Castlerigg that he hadn't really thought about the return journey at all.

He suddenly felt very disheartened; his shoulders

slumped and he looked really miserable. 'I'm sorry, David,' he said glumly, 'I didn't think about how we were going to get home again. I suppose the only thing we could do is find the nearest police station and turn ourselves in. We'll be in an awful lot of trouble if we do that, but at least the police would see we got home safely. Maybe they'd phone our parents and ask them to come and get us.

'Anyway, we don't even know if our plan is going to work, do we? The portal might not be there. Menhir might not get back to Dragonworld after all, and then I'll have got you into all sorts of trouble for nothing.'

David swallowed the last bite of his burger, then wiped his fingers on the tissue that came with it.

'Don't you think I know that, Tim? You didn't ask me to come with you; that was my idea. I came because you're my friend. We share our time, our play, our money and our food. If there's going to be trouble I'll share that too, because that's what friends are for.'

Timothy managed a sheepish smile. 'I'm glad you came with me, David.'

The little dragon popped his head out of the trolley bag for a moment to look once more at the faces of the small humans who were trying so hard to help him. Then he went back to finish his tray of salmon dog food, keeping his thoughts to himself.

David got up, collected the coffee cups, burger boxes, and the empty tray from the trolley bag, then dropped them into a nearby waste bin. While his back was turned, Timothy quickly wiped his eyes on the sleeve of his hoody.

Chapter 12: The Teacher and the Basket

They were too excited to sleep on the train to Penrith, so they sat looking out of the window, talking over what they had accomplished so far, and what they thought the next few hours might bring.

'You were going to tell me about that dream,' said David.

Timothy told his friend all that he could remember about the dream; about the great stone circle, the people working there, and the man who had called himself Kannith.

'Who was Kannith, Tim?'

'I don't know. He didn't tell me, and there wasn't time to ask him. He might have been the leader of those people; a sort of Chief or something. Or maybe he was a Druid. I'll tell you something, though.'

'What's that?'

'Menhir said that he'd only met one other person like me in his whole life. I don't know what he meant by that, but I'm willing to bet the other person was Kannith. Am I right, Menhir?'

'Yes, Timothy,' said the dragon, 'you are perfectly correct.'

Timothy looked at his friend. 'I don't know what's so special about me, though, David. You're the clever one. Everyone knows you're the best in the school at maths.'

David shrugged. 'Yeah, and they know you're the best at most everything else. My dad says I ought to be an accountant when I grow up. He says accountants earn a lot of money. What about you?'

'I think I'd like to be an archaeologist. You know, the people who dig things up and find out about the past.'

As the little dragon listened, he was going through the memory pictures in Timothy's mind. He stopped when he came across the memories of a boy called Dennis Parker. There were quite a lot of those memories, and he looked at them very carefully.

'Hmm,' he thought, 'I won't be able to do anything about that myself, but I think I know someone who will.'

The boys took their hoodies off because the day was becoming very warm, stuffed them down into David's backpack, then drank some of the water from the two drinker bottles.

Penrith station turned out to be very different from Manchester Piccadilly. It was very old-fashioned looking, and here, there were no shops at all. There was a small café on the platform, though, where they bought two packs of sandwiches and another bottle of water.

There were no automatic ticket barriers either, and the man checking tickets at the gate between the platform and the exit didn't even look at them as they walked through.

On the pavement outside the station they found

themselves facing the ruins of Penrith castle. 'There's a bus stop just over there,' said David pointing to his left. We might be able to get a bus to Castlerigg.'

They were just about to step out for the bus stop when a voice from behind them said, 'Hello, boys! What are you doing here?'

Their hearts in their mouths, they turned around. Standing right behind them was Mr Tennison, the sports master from the high school they were going to after the holidays. 'You must have been on the same train as me,' he said, 'but I didn't notice you until you got off.' He looked at David's backpack and the trolley.

'Going camping, are you? Well, this is a really lovely area for it. And that's s pretty smart idea you've got there: carrying your camping gear in a shopping trolley.'

Timothy's brain went into overdrive. 'Um, yes, Mr Tennison. We're, er, we're going to meet a friend of a friend at Castlerigg stone circle.'

It wasn't really a lie because, although they didn't know the name of the dragon that they hoped would come through the portal to rescue Menhir, it wouldn't exactly be an enemy, and it would certainly be a friend of Menhir's.

'Oh, the famous stone circle, eh?' said Mr Tennison. 'Well now, that's really worth seeing. Are you boys interested in history?'

'Yes sir, we are,' replied Timothy. 'We were just going to see if we could find a bus to take us there.'

'Oh, you needn't worry about that. There should be a hire car waiting for me in the station car park. I've just got to go and sign the hire papers and pick up the keys. Just wait here, I'll be back in a moment. I'm on my way to Keswick, so I'll drop you off close to the stone circle.'

Very soon, the boys were in Mr Tennison's hired car travelling along the A66 towards Keswick. Mr Tennison had suggested that they should put the trolley in the car's boot, but Timothy said, 'Can I stand it in front of the back seat, please? There's things in there that might spill if we lay it down.' The teacher readily agreed: they would only be using one of the backs seats anyway.

David did his best to suppress a grin as he gave his friend a nod. It would have been very hot and stuffy in the boot, and extremely uncomfortable for the little dragon if he'd been shut in there.

'So, you boys are interested in history, are you?' the sports teacher asked as he drove along.

'Yes,' replied David, 'but we're interested in learning to play tennis, too.'

A smile broke out on Mr Tennison's face. 'That's very good to know. At lunchtime on your first day at High School, come and find me. I'll be in the main hall taking the names of those who want to join the after-school tennis club. The club's only been going for a year, and so far, we've only got ten members. A couple of new faces would be most welcome.'

'Ok, thank you, Mr Tennison,' said Timothy. 'We'll

be there. Are you on holiday too?'

'As a matter of fact,' said Mr Tennison, 'I'm here to see a teacher friend of mine. She teaches sports at the school in Keswick. She's very keen on tennis, too.'

Still on the main A66, not far from where the sports teacher was going to drop them off, they passed a big sign at the side of the road. It read, 'Lakeland Balloon Centre'. Looking out through the car windows they saw two hot air balloons that had just taken off. The people riding in the baskets slung underneath the balloons were waving to them. David slid his side window down and waved back.

Timothy noticed that underneath the sign stood a big wickerwork basket, just like the ones the balloon people were riding in. He also noticed that a few fluffy white clouds had appeared in the sky. It had been clear blue sky all day up until then, and he began to worry that it might turn cloudy. 'If it does,' he thought, 'there won't be a bright moon, and all our trouble will have been for nothing.'

'We're going to see if we can arrange a tennis match between my school team and hers,' Mr Tennison went on. 'Of course, it would mean my team coming up here to stay in Keswick for a few days, but it would count as an educational trip, you see.'

'Oh, wow!' said David. 'That sounds great, Mr Tennison. Would we be able to go with the team?'

'If you turn out to be good players, yes, that's entirely possible. We'll need good players to beat the Keswick school team.'

A few minutes later, the sports teacher pulled over to the side of the road and stopped the car.

'This is where I drop you off, lads,' he said. 'The stone circle is just …'

'Down Castle Lane,' said David, looking at his tablet computer. 'That's just a mile to the south of where we are now.'

'Well, I'm impressed with you two,' said Mr Tennison. 'You lads are well organised. If you can play tennis to the same standard, our team's sure to win!'

The boys climbed out of the car, shook hands with the teacher and thanked him for his help.

'Good luck, lads. I hope you have a very enjoyable camping trip, and that the weather stays fine for you.'

Following the Walkway app on David's tablet, the boys turned left into a road called Burns. When they were out of sight, the sports teacher put the car into gear and drove away down the road towards Keswick.

Chapter 13: The Portal

Although David had been right when he said the stone circle was only a mile from where Mr Tennison had dropped them off, the boys soon discovered that there was no way they could walk in a straight line from there to Castlerigg. Following the directions of the Walkway app on David's tablet, they walked on along Burns even though it meant that they were moving further away from the stone circle.

'It's okay,' said David, 'this is the right way to get there. We'll come to a turning on our right before long, and then another right turn. After that we'll be in a road called Eleventrees. The gate that lets you into the field where the stone circle is, is in that road, and not Castle Lane after all.'

It was a hot day, and the boys were soon tired. They stopped to rest a couple of times, so it was almost four o'clock in the afternoon when they finally saw the National Trust sign that stands by the gate in the dry stone wall that leads to Castlerigg.

'There doesn't seem to be anyone else here,' said Timothy, as they walked across the grassy field towards the great stones.

'In that case,' came the squeaky voice, 'perhaps you could let me out. I think I've been in this stuffy bag long enough.'

When Timothy unzipped the top of the trolley bag,

Menhir jumped out onto the grass.

'Ooh,' he said, 'I've been longing to get out of there. I need to stretch my wings. Don't worry, if anyone sees me from a distance, they'll think I'm an eagle.'

With that, he leaped into the air. Flying round and round in an upward spiral, he gradually gained height until he was just a tiny speck way up in the sky.

The boys watched him for a few moments, then found themselves a spot where they could sit in shade with their backs against one of the upright stones. There was almost no wind at all that day, but Timothy thought the clouds were moving very slowly, and that there were more of them than there had been earlier.

Both boys were hungry again by that time. They agreed to eat one of the packs of sandwiches, and to save the other pack for the morning. There were more clouds in the sky by that time, and some of them were beginning to look rather grey. Menhir returned from his flight to perch on top of the stone.

'I don't like the look of that sky very much,' said Timothy. 'If those clouds cover the moon tonight, the portal won't form, will it, Menhir?'

'Don't worry, Timothy,' replied the dragon. 'We dragons have an instinct about these things. It's possible that everything might turn out better than you expect.'

They spent a while wandering around the stone circle, looking at the stones, and at the hills around them, but they spent most of the next three or four hours just sitting still, worried about what they would do if things didn't turn out well.

At last the sky began to grow dark. By that time, grey clouds had covered the whole sky, but they could tell that the moon had started to rise because they could see it glowing behind the clouds. The air had turned damp, as though it was going to rain. Moments later, a fine drizzle began to dampen their hoodies.

'It's not going to work, is it, Menhir? There's too much cloud. The moon won't be bright enough.'

'Look over to the west, Timothy,' answered the dragon. 'Look, there's a break in the clouds, and it's moving this way.'

A few minutes later, the moon broke through the grey clouds: bright and full, bathing the stone circle with silver light. Although it hadn't risen very far above the horizon, it looked unusually large. In the clear patch of sky around the moon bright stars were shining as the drizzle from the grey clouds continued to fall.

'Look!' David called out. 'There's a ring forming around the moon!'

Timothy looked up to see that there were two rings. The ring nearest the moon was yellow. The one a little further out was orange.

'It's a moonbow! A moonbow!' shouted Timothy excitedly. He was practically jumping up and down. Menhir had flown up to sit on top of the tall stone where the boys had been sitting.

As they watched, something quite unexpected happened. One moment, it had been two faint rings of

120

light, one orange and one yellow. But in the space of a split second, it had changed colour.

'Look! Look!' cried Timothy, 'It's turned blue! The moonbow's turned blue!'

As the moonbow changed colour, it began to revolve slowly, its edges becoming ragged as it turned, and it seemed be dragging the whole sky and the grey clouds around with it, just like the laundry in his mother's washing machine before it did a spin. The glow of the moon became even brighter, as it, too, began to revolve, becoming a dazzling, white light at the centre of a whirlpool in the sky.

'Surely, Menhir, people must be able to see this all over the country,' said David.

'No, David, they can't. You can only see the portal if you are standing in the stone circle. If you look from anywhere else, all you see is the moonbow, and then you can't tell if a portal has opened or not. That's why us dragons had to make the stone circles, you see, because you can't see a portal unless you're standing in the right spot.'

As the boys stared upwards, their mouths open in wonder, the sky above them suddenly went dark. It seemed as though someone had flicked a switch and turned the moon and stars off. Slowly, they realised that the reason they couldn't see the moon and stars anymore was because a huge, black shape was hanging above them, slowly flapping its enormous wings. It was so big that it seemed to blot out the entire night sky.

'Rhyol! It's Rhyol!' Menhir called out. But instead of landing on the ground, the massive shape rose upwards, its huge wings propelling it at speed across the night sky, as it flew rapidly away towards the east.

'Where's he going?' Timothy yelled. 'Rhyol! Rhyol, we're here! Down here!'

'It's all right, Timothy,' said Menhir. 'Rhyol has read the images in my mind, and yours, and David's, too. He knows who you are and what you've done to help me. He knows exactly what to do, and he'll be back in a few minutes. Watch the sky to the east.'

'Can dragons really do it that quickly?' asked David.

'Oh, yes,' replied the little dragon, 'We can read dozens of mind pictures in just a few seconds. It's as easy for us to do that as it is for you to speak to Timothy, but we do it much faster.'

It seemed to the boys that they stood there in the stone circle, with the burning light of the portal shining above them, for ages. But it was really only a few minutes before they saw the dark shape of the huge dragon returning swiftly against the backdrop of swirling grey clouds. He was carrying something in his huge talons. As he drew closer, they could see that it was the basket from the balloon centre that they had passed on the main road.

Rhyol descended until the bottom of the basket touched the ground.

'Quickly now, boys,' said Menhir. 'Climb into the basket. Hurry, there's not much time. Get the trolley. That must come too.' As he said it, he flew up onto the back of the basket, gripping onto the edge so that he was facing the same way as Rhyol.

David, still wearing his backpack, scrambled up and over the side. Timothy grabbed the trolley, passed it up to him, then seized the edge of the basket while David hauled him in. As soon as he tumbled aboard, the great dragon soared up into the sky, spiralling round and round to gain height before heading straight towards the portal, his great talons gripping the basket so tightly that his claws pierced right through the sides.

As they passed into the swirling mouth of the portal, a howling wind began to roar around them. The basket shook, and swayed, and bucked from side to side as the wind screamed and tore at their hair and clothes as though it would rip them from safety and hurl them out into the whirlpool of light that surrounded them.

Crouching in the bottom of the basket, clinging on to the wickerwork for dear life, they could see the gigantic wings of the great stone dragon above them, pulling and straining against the wind to get them through the tunnel of light. Menhir, on the back edge of the basket, was flapping his wings as hard as he could.

And then, as suddenly as it began, the wind was gone. They stood up to peer over the sides of the balloon basket. There below them, under the glare of a portal moon and a clear night sky absolutely covered with millions of stars, was the fantastic landscape of Dragonworld.

A seemingly endless ocean stretched to the horizon in

every direction, and in that ocean were dozens of islands; some big, and some small. Several of the smaller islands had volcanoes on them, their tops glowing with red and orange flames as the heat from the fire in their hearts, and the steam from where molten lava flowed into the sea, rose way up into the air.

'It's exactly like the image you put in my mind, Menhir,' said Timothy as he twisted around to look where the little dragon had been crouching. But the space where Menhir had been was empty.

'Where's Menhir, David? Where did he go?'

'Look over there,' replied David, 'back towards the portal. I think that's him.'

Timothy turned around in the basket to face back the way they had come. The glowing white portal was still there. Silhouetted against its light, another huge stone dragon was rushing towards them. Timothy knew straight away that David was right. It *was* Menhir, but he was no longer a miniature dragon: he was back to his full size. As he flew up alongside the basket he called out, 'It's all right, Timothy. It's me, Menhir. As soon as we came through the portal I had to jump out of the basket because I knew that, once I was back in Dragonworld, I would be my true size again.'

Timothy wanted to ask how that had happened, but even as Menhir spoke, Rhyol banked around and began to head back towards the portal as fast as his great wings could drive the basket along.

'There's no time, Timothy!' Menhir called out as they flew away. 'There's no time to explain! You must go back through the portal before it closes! Goodbye, and thank you for everything you've done!'

By the time Menhir had finished speaking, they were already rushing headlong back into the portal's tunnel of swirling light. This time, with the howling wind behind them, they zoomed through the portal in seconds, and were back in the air above the stone circle almost before they realised it. The boys didn't even have time to ask Menhir why they couldn't stay in Dragonworld a bit longer.

Instead of setting the basket down on the ground, Rhyol spiralled up higher into the sky and began to beat his massive wings even more strongly as he headed south, away from Castlerigg, as fast as he could fly.

Looking back towards the portal, Timothy saw that a cloud had moved across the moon, so that he could no longer see it. He didn't expect to see the portal because Menhir had said that it was only visible from inside the stone circle, so he couldn't tell whether it was still open or not.

Chapter 14: Home in Time

'Rhyol should have dropped us back in the stone circle, shouldn't he?' said David with a worried look on his face. 'Where's he taking us?'

Timothy looked down over the side of the basket. Already the lights of Keswick were far behind them, while ahead, was the beginning of an orange glow in the sky that might have been the northern lights of Leeds or Bradford.

Timothy was about to say that he didn't know, when a picture of his own house suddenly came into his head, and he realised that it was Rhyol who had put it there.

'Home, David, that's where! Rhyol's taking us home!'

The dragon was flying so fast that a strong, cold wind was buffeting them around their heads and shoulders. David pulled Timothy's sleeping back out of the trolley. It was one those sleeping bags that unzipped all the all way around so it could be opened up like a double-sized duvet. The boys huddled down in the basket, wrapping the unzipped sleeping bag around themselves.

'Rhyol's going as fast as a train,' said Timothy,' but even so, it's still going to take a few hours to get home. We might as well sleep if we can.'

'How's Rhyol going to get home, then? It'll be the best part of a whole day before he gets back to Castlerigg, won't it? The portal will have closed long before that.'

'I don't know, David. But I know this: dragons are clever. They know things we don't. We'll just have to trust that they know what they're doing.'

'We're going to be in all sorts of trouble when we get back, though, aren't we?' said David. 'Our parents will be going frantic wondering where we've gone. They'll be angry. They'll have the police out looking for us. There'll be blue lights flashing all over the place.'

'Yeah, I know,' said Timothy. 'I feel badly about making my parents worry. I didn't want to upset them. I just wanted to get Menhir home.'

'Well, we've done that, haven't we, Tim? And I'll tell you this: whatever happens next, I don't think I'll ever be sorry we did it.'

Timothy turned his head towards his friend and grinned. 'No, nor will I.'

As the basket rocked gently from side to side, and the great dragon continued his journey south, the boys, now warmly wrapped up in the sleeping bag, fell into a deep sleep.

When they woke up, they looked down to find that, although it was still dark, they could tell from the shape of the river, the roads, and the street lights, that they were over Oxford. The basket seemed to be descending.

'Hey!' David called out, 'Isn't that Dennis Parker's house down there? Look: there, in that side road off Cumnore Hill.'

'Erm, yes, I think it is!' replied Timothy.

Rhyol banked around in a circle above Dennis's house for about half a minute, and then he flew on. After a few moments, they could see Timothy's house and garden.

'I don't see any blue lights anywhere,' said David. 'It all looks very quiet down there.'

'There's no lights on in my house either,' answered Timothy, 'or in any of the neighbours' houses. Maybe they're all out looking for us.'

As the basket bumped gently down in Timothy's back garden, he got a picture from Rhyol that said they must hurry because he had to fly straight back to Castlerigg, and there wasn't a moment to lose. The boys dropped the trolley over the side, threw the sleeping bag after it, and jumped out onto the lawn.

As soon as were they were clear of the basket, Rhyol flapped his great wings, spiralling back up into the air with such speed that, in just a couple of minutes, he was already disappearing into the cloudy sky.

'Hey, look, David,' said Timothy, 'the tent's still here. I'd have thought my dad would have taken it down when he found we were gone.'

'Maybe he just hasn't had time. Perhaps he's been too busy looking for you.'

'Maybe. Let's get my sleeping bag back in the tent,

anyway.'

As they laid the sleeping bag back in its place, Timothy picked up his alarm clock. 'I think it must have stopped,' he said. 'It still says five o'clock.'

After he said that, he froze, kneeling on the tent floor, while his brain went into overdrive. He looked up at his friend. 'David, what day is it?'

'Well, it was the twenty-sixth yesterday when we set out, so it must be the twenty-seventh now.'

'That's odd. If this is the night of the twenty-seventh, then we must have slept all day and all night in that basket on the way back from Castlerigg. But I don't think we did. David … what does your tablet say?'

'I suppose it must say … Wait a minute, something must have gone wrong with it. It says today's date is the twenty-sixth. That can't be right, can it?'

Timothy suddenly felt a bit dizzy. 'Give me a moment to think, David. I'm just going to put mum's trolley back where I found it. I won't be a minute.'

When he came back David was lying down on his sleeping back just as he had been before they left. 'David,' he said, 'I've been thinking. You remember what Menhir said about the portals – that they always lead to the same place, but not always to the same time?'

'Yes, I think so.'

'Well, I think Menhir and Rhyol knew *exactly* what they were doing. Rhyol didn't have to take us through the portal at all. He could have just taken Menhir

130

back to Dragonworld in the basket, and left us where we were, couldn't he?'

'I suppose so.'

'So why did he do it? Why did he take us too?'

David shrugged. 'Maybe he just thought we'd like to see Dragonworld. I certainly enjoyed it, anyway, and I'm sure you did.'

'That may be true, but I think there was another reason. They knew that if we went through the portal just for – what was it? – a minute or two? then, when we came back, it would be at a different time from when went we went in. Not different by just a few minutes, but by a whole day. That's why Menhir wouldn't let us stay in Dragonworld any longer than we did.'

'You mean … not different by a day *later*, but different by a day *earlier*?'

'Yes, David, that has to be it! Come outside. Come out and look at the moon.'

They stood on the lawn together, looking up at the sky.

'Do you see it, David? Do you see it?'

'Yes, I do. The moon has just a little bit missing. It's the day *before* a full moon. It means that today really *is* the twenty-sixth of August, and that there'll be a full moon tonight.'

'That's right. So, when Rhyol gets back to Castlerigg tonight, the moon will be full, the portal will open, just like it did when we were there, and he'll be able to fly straight home again, back to Dragonworld. We *know* it's going to open for him because we've already seen it.'

They looked at each other and burst out laughing.

'So, there won't be any trouble for us at all because, as far as our parents are concerned, we've never been away. So far as they'll ever know, we just spent a night in this tent on the lawn like we said we were going to. Menhir's safely back where he belongs, and Rhyol will be home, too, very soon. Dragons aren't daft, are they?'

'Do you think we'll ever see them again, Tim?'

'I've got a feeling we will. Maybe not this year, maybe not next. But one day, yes. One day, I'm sure we will.'

'What makes you so certain?'

'Because they didn't make us forget.'

Epilogue: First Day Surprises

On the first day of the new term, David arrived at the High School early. There was no sign of Timothy. As he walked up the school driveway, the first person he met was Dennis Parker. He didn't recognise Dennis at first, because he was smartly dressed in school uniform with polished black shoes and a school tie.

'Hi, David,' said Dennis in a pleasant voice. 'Did you have a good holiday?'

David couldn't believe either his eyes or his ears.

'This isn't the Dennis Parker I used to know,' thought David. 'I wonder if he had an accident during the holidays? Maybe he fell over and banged his head on something.'

'You're looking very smart, Dennis,' he said.

'Oh, thanks. My mother thought I ought to have a proper uniform. My two elder brothers have moved out. The older one got a job on the oil rigs up in Scotland, and the middle one suddenly decided to join the Army. They weren't working before, you see, and they always kept mum short of money. Now that they've gone, she's much better off.'

'Um ... so, you're the youngest brother, then?'

'Yeah, that's right. Didn't I ever tell you? They used to make my life really miserable; always bullying me and knocking me around. They used to think it was

133

fun.'

'You're not going to miss them very much, then?'

Dennis laughed. 'Are you kidding? I'm glad they're both gone.'

Timothy walked up the drive to join them.

'Hi David,' he said cheerfully.

Dennis looked at David. 'Who's this new kid? Do you know him, David?'

'It's Timothy Tamworth,' he said pointing at Timothy. 'He was in our class in Junior School. Don't you remember him?'

'No, I can't say I do.' Dennis reached out his hand to Timothy. 'Hello, Timothy,' he said, 'Nice to meet you. Are we all going to be in the same class, do you think?

Timothy took Dennis's hand and shook it, mainly because doing that stopped him from falling over backwards. Like David, he couldn't believe what he was seeing or hearing. Not only had Dennis's manner and way of dressing changed, his voice had changed, too. He was no longer the rough, tough playground bully, but a well-spoken, smartly dressed and very likeable young man.

'Let go in and find out, shall we, Dennis?' he said.

They followed a sign that directed new pupils to the reception room, which turned out to be a large library. Ten tables had been arranged around the room in informal fashion, with four chairs to each table. The tables were filling up with groups of friends, but they quickly found an empty one at the side of the room.

No sooner had they sat down than an athletic-looking girl, with long dark hair tied back in a pony tail, pulled out the fourth chair and sat down with them. None of them had ever seen her before.

'Hi,' said David. 'I'm David Westfield, and this is Timothy Tamworth and Dennis Parker.'

The girl opened her school bag, pulled out a note pad and pen, and laid them on the table in front of her.

'Yes, I know,' she replied. 'That's to say, I know you and Tamworth.

'How come? We don't know you, do we, Tim?'

'Mr Tennison told me you want to learn to play tennis.'

'Are you going to learn too?'

'Learn? No, I can already play. I've heard there's an after-school tennis club here. Are you going to join?'

'Yes, we are,' said Timothy, 'Mr Tennison will be taking the names of those who want to join in the hall at lunchtime.'

On a sudden impulse, he said, 'Why don't you come and sign up too, Dennis? Mr Tennison would be pleased to get some extra members for the club.'

'Me? I've never played tennis. I'm more of a football fan. Well … that's not really true. I've never played football either, not in a team or a club or anything. I always had to pretend to be a football fan or my brothers would've … well, you know … they would've …'

'It's ok, Dennis,' said David, 'you're among friends now. Look, come along and sign up with us. Tennis is a great game. You have to be really fit to play it well. And being a member of a club is good fun. You'll like it.'

'Dennis grinned and shrugged. 'Yeah, ok. Why not?'

'So,' said the girl, 'there's four of us, then.'

Timothy looked at her.

'Um, you didn't say what your name is.'

'Oh, I'm Cathy Gilson. I'm the Girls' Under-Thirteen Hampshire County tennis champion. My family moved to Oxford four weeks ago.'

Timothy's school tennis team went to Keswick in the spring of the following year. They beat the Keswick team, in a ten-match tournament, by seven matches to three. David and Timothy both won their singles matches, while Dennis and Cathy slammed their opponents a to a straight-sets defeat, by winning all four* of their sets in the mixed doubles match.

When the group made a visit to Castlerigg, Timothy gave them a talk about stone circles. He didn't say anything about dragons though, because no one would have believed him.

*By agreement between the two teachers, because the players were juniors, they played four sets to a match instead of the six sets that adults play.

Printed in Great Britain
by Amazon